·El Toro & Friends·

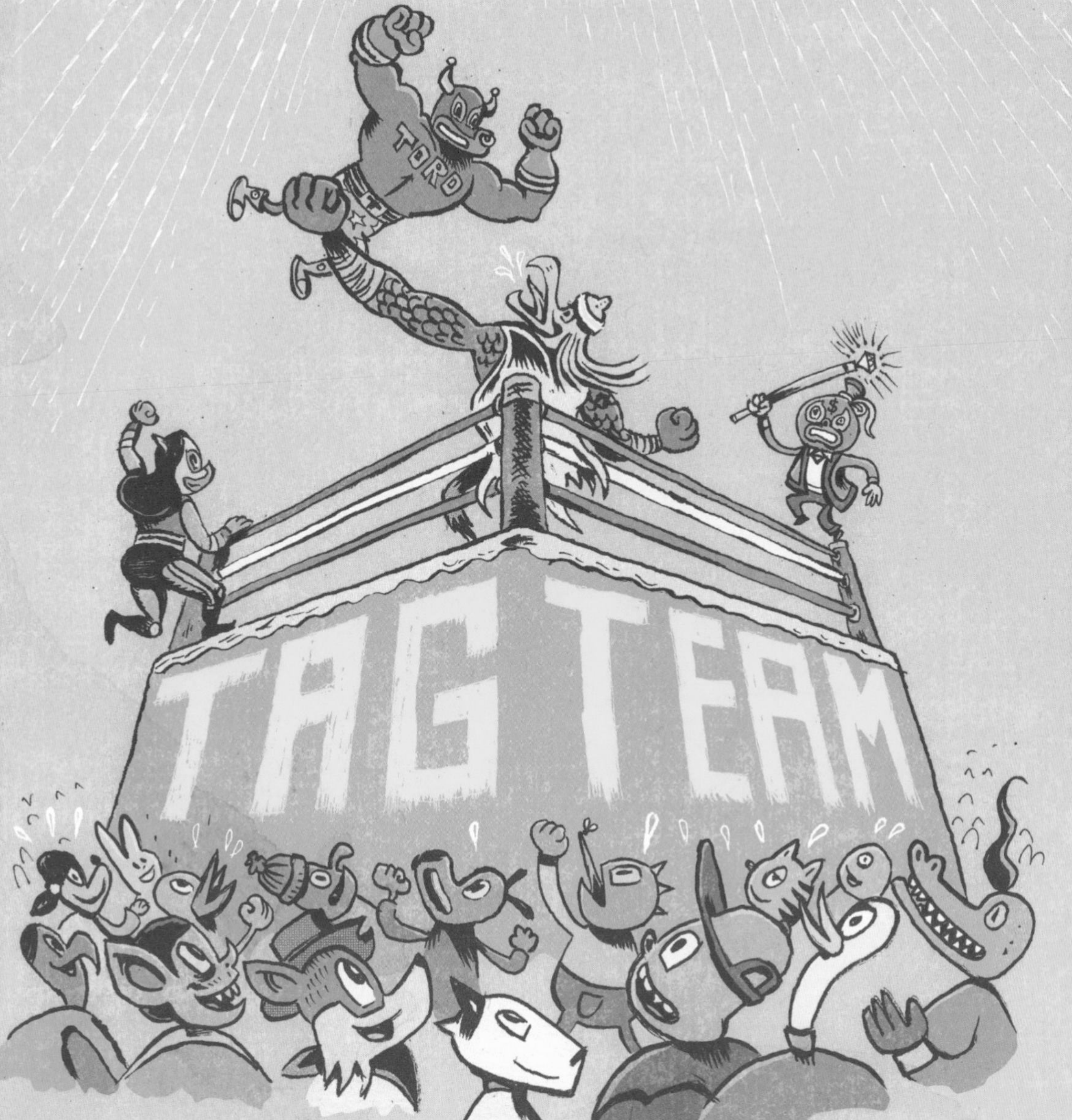
TORO
TAG TEAM

by Raúl the Third
colors by Elaine Bay

VERSIFY
Imprints of HarperCollinsPublishers
HARPER alley

Last night was exciting.
El Coliseo rattled and shook
with cheers and boos!

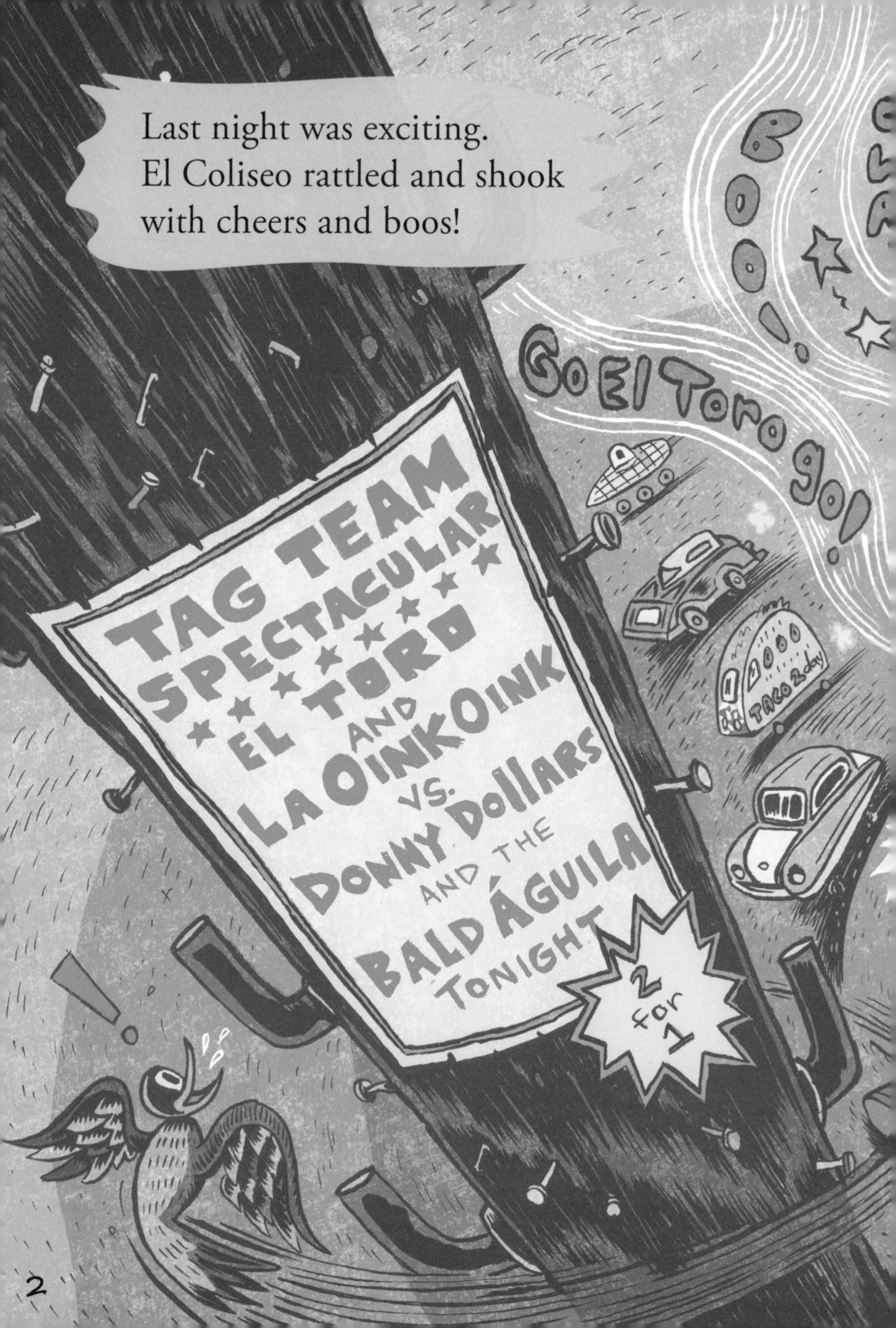
BOO!
Go El Toro go!
TAG TEAM
SPECTACULAR
EL TORO
AND
LA OINK OINK
VS.
DONNY DOLLARS
AND THE
BALD ÁGUILA
TONIGHT
2 for 1
TACO 2 day

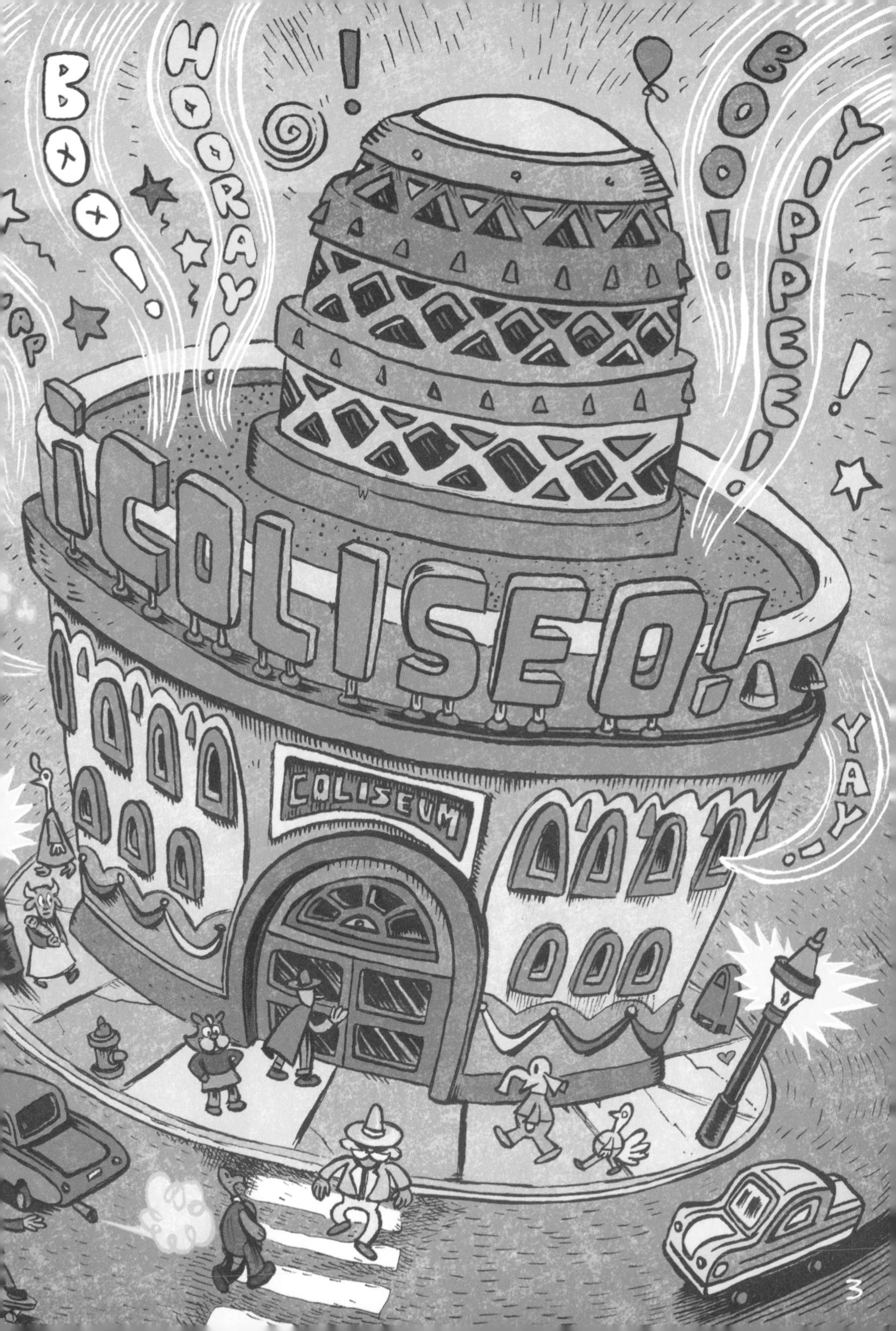
BOO!
HOORAY!
BOO!
YIPPEE!
¡COLISEO!
COLISEUM
YAY

El Toro and La Oink Oink battled
Donny Dollars and the Bald Águila
for the Tag Team Championship.

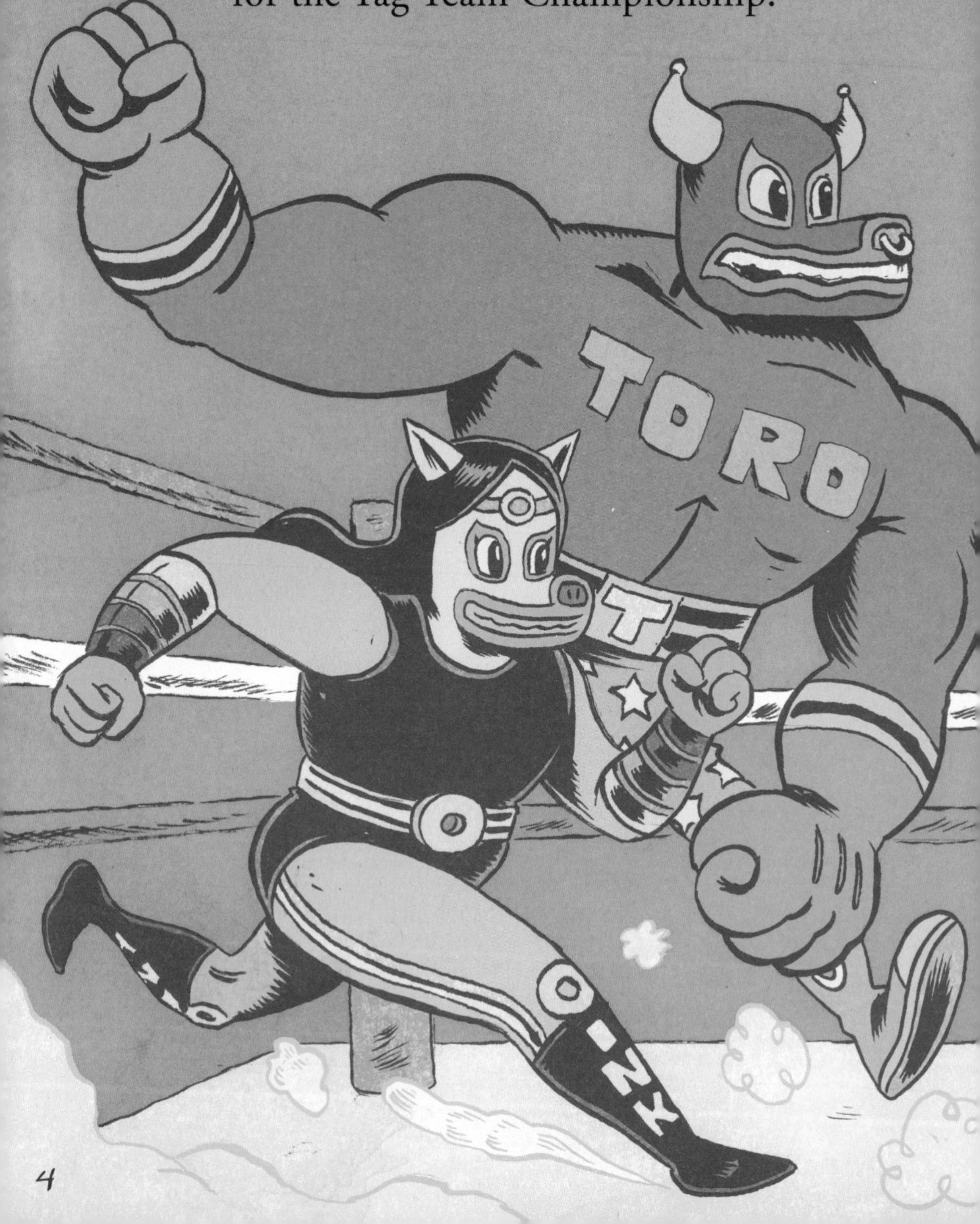
TORO
OINK

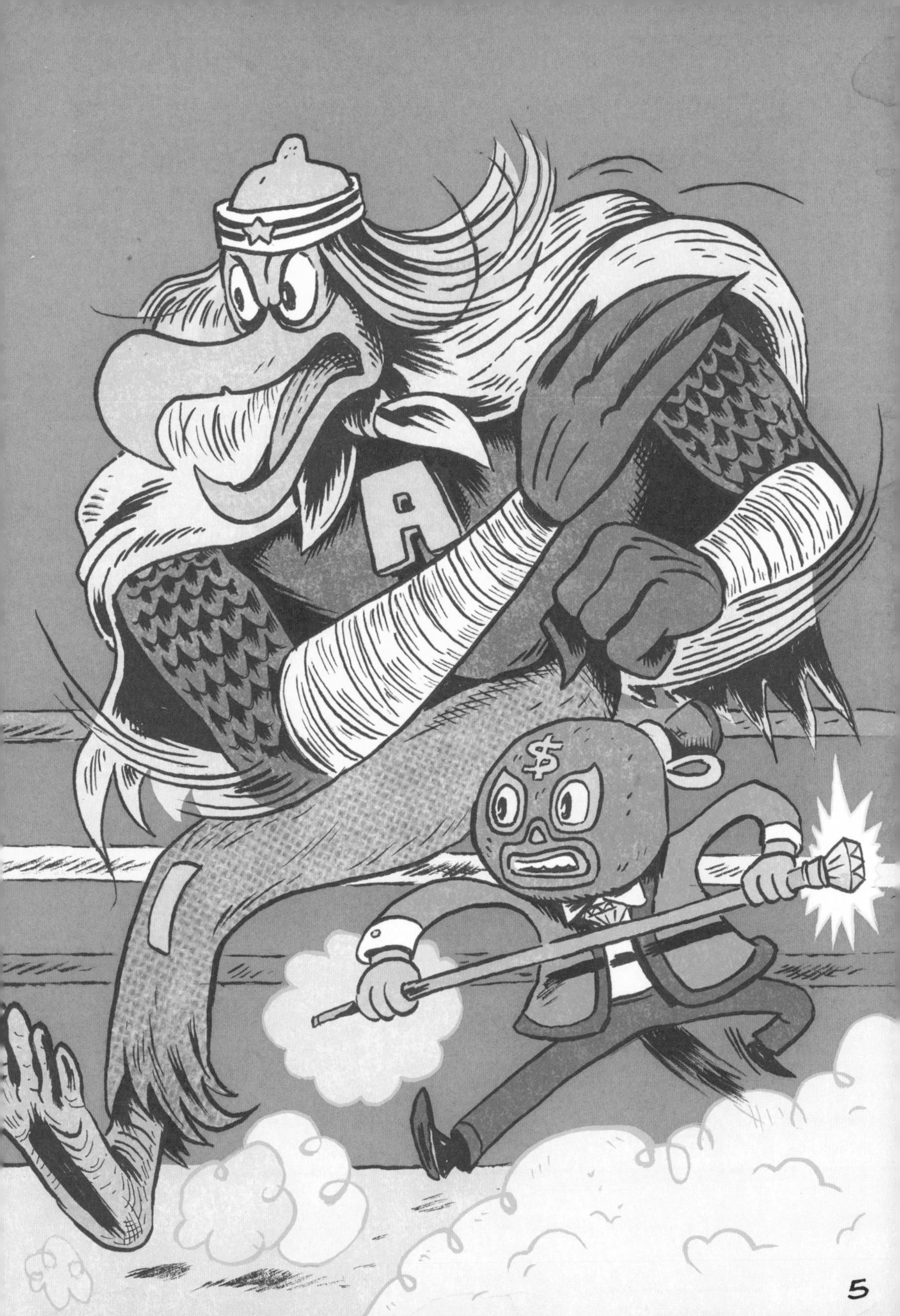

When El Toro needed help with the Bald Águila, he tagged La Oink Oink.

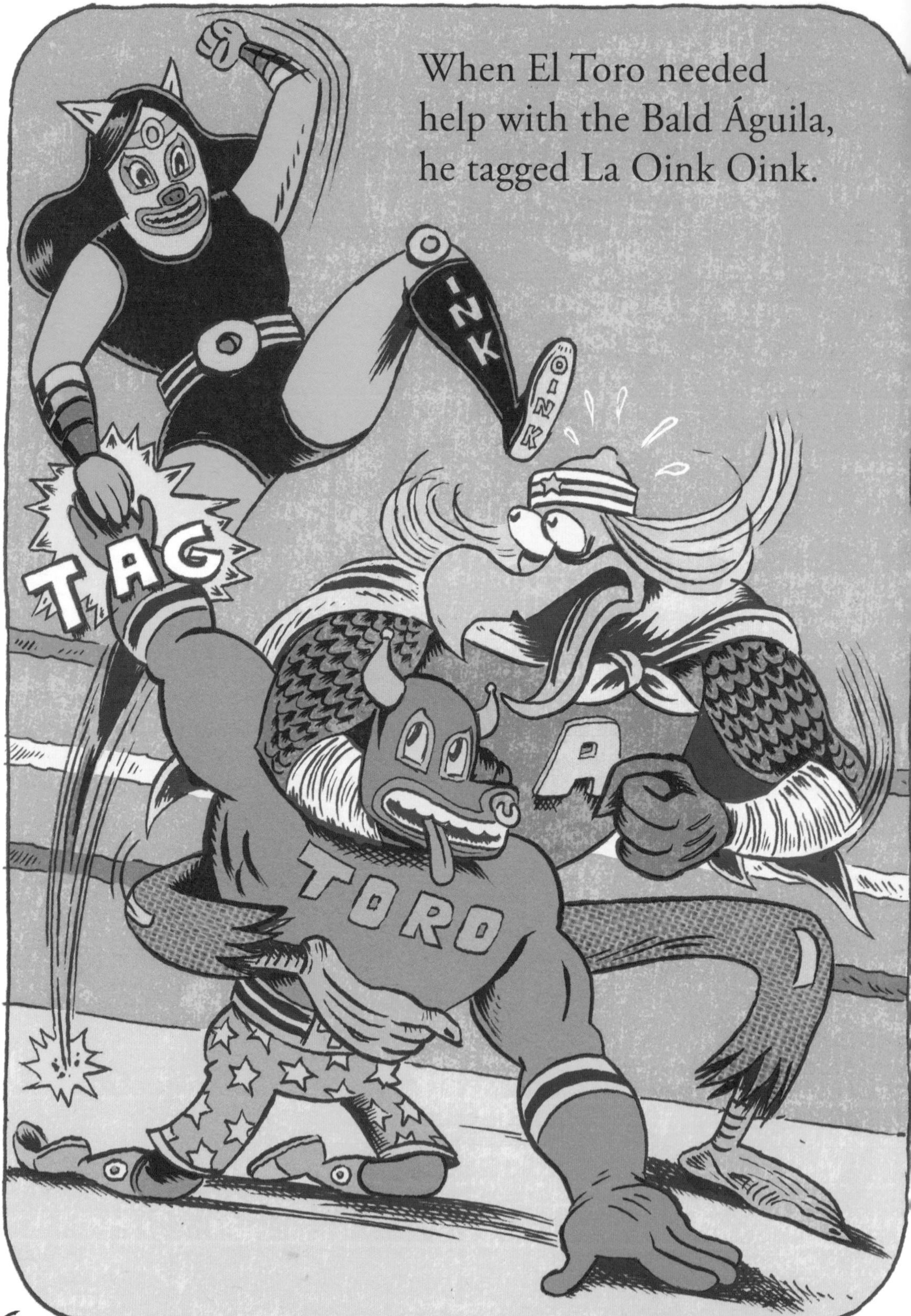
INK
OINK
TAG
A
TORO

The Bald Águila tagged Donny Dollars for help with La Oink Oink. The match lasted for hours!

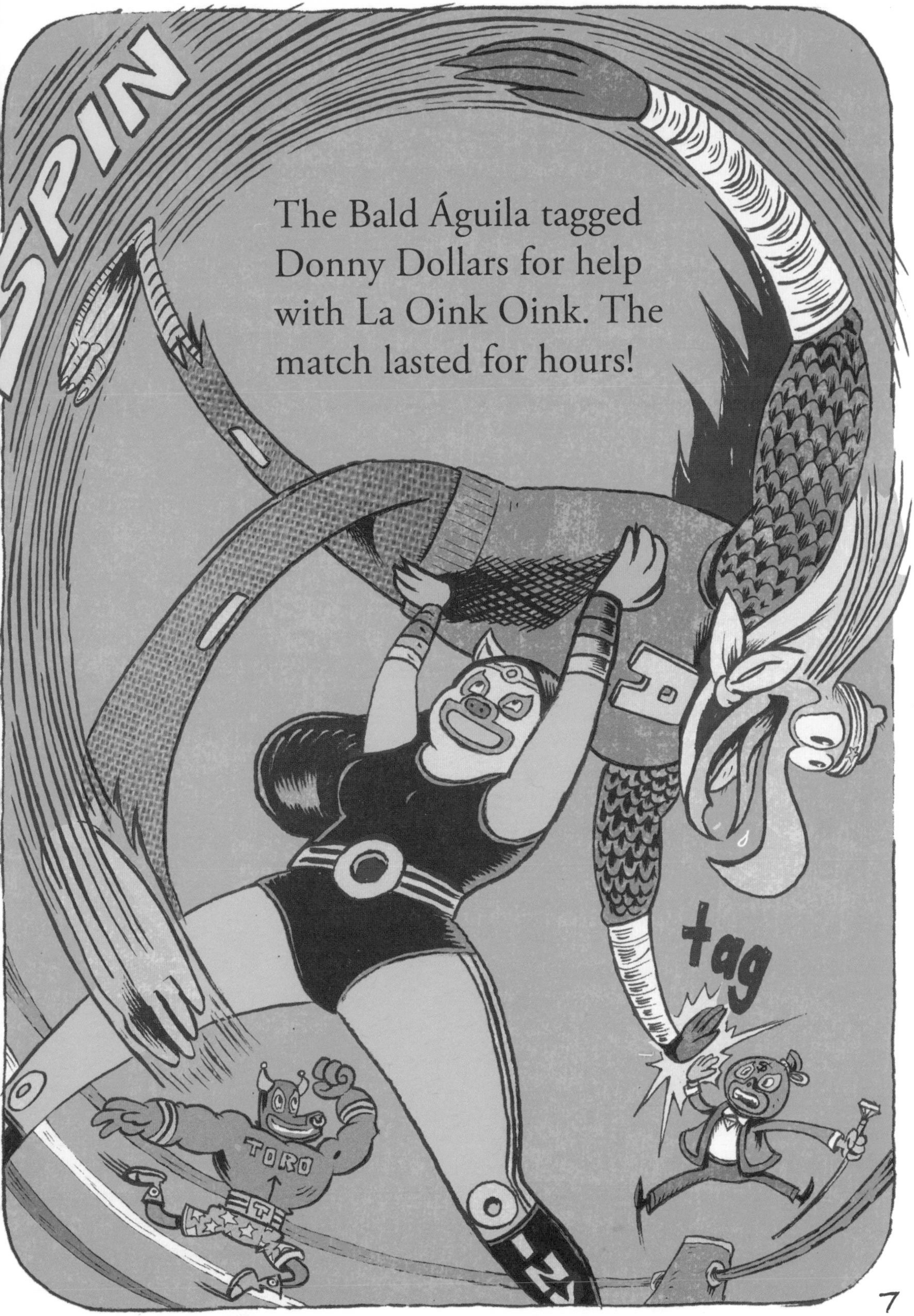
SPIN
tag
TORO

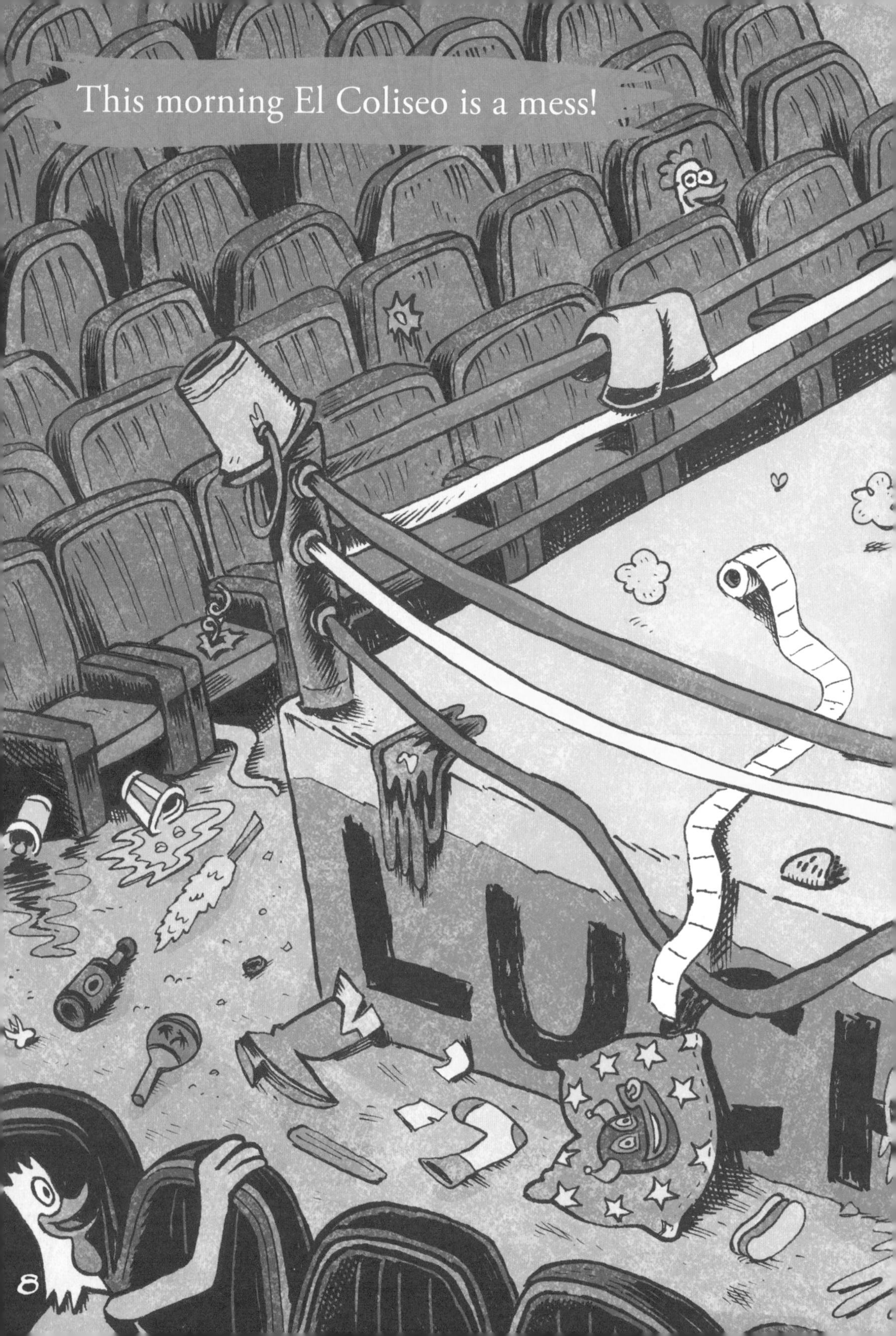
This morning El Coliseo is a mess!

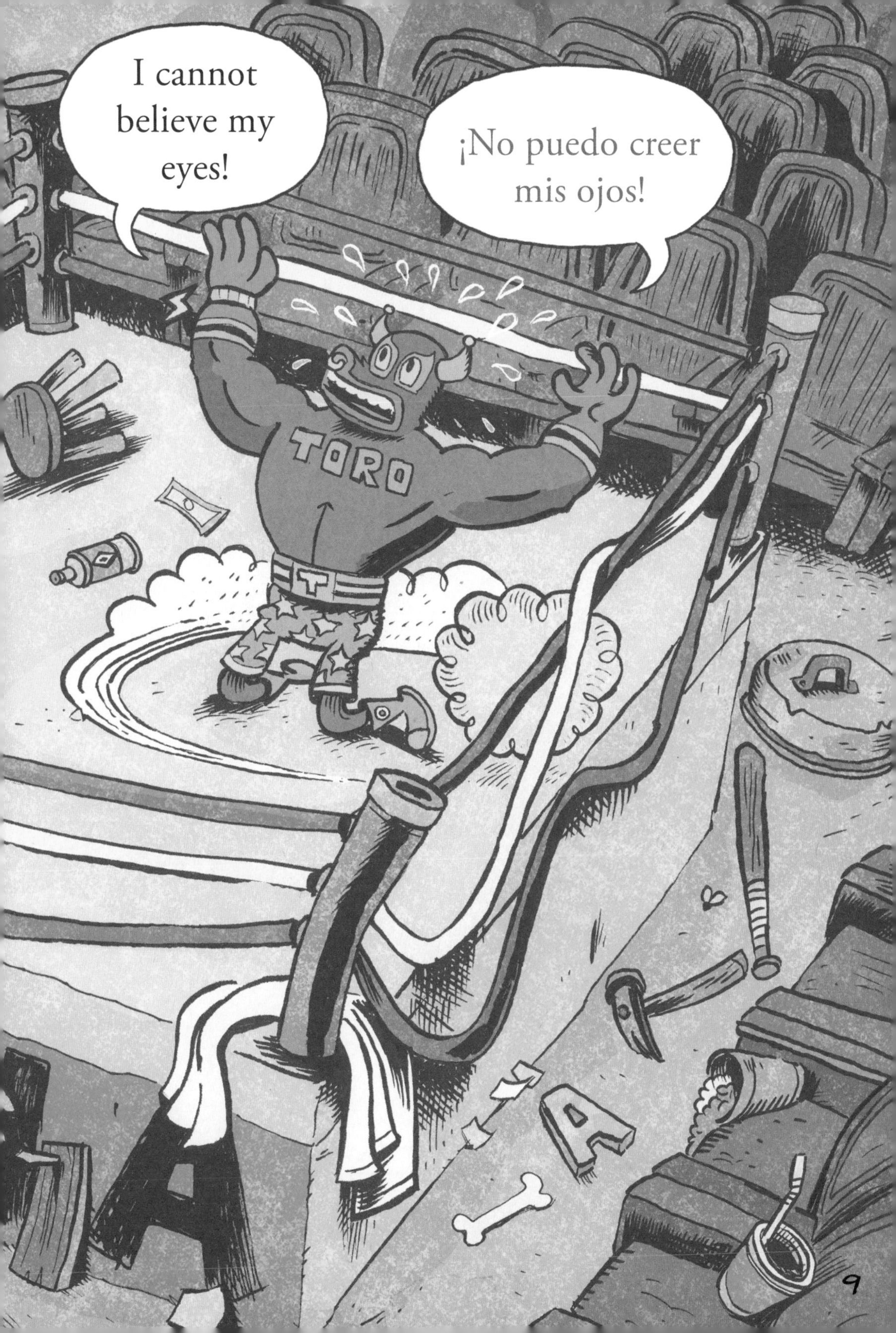
I cannot believe my eyes!
¡No puedo creer mis ojos!
TORO
T
A
A

Mal Burro and Peeky Pequeño are not coming in.

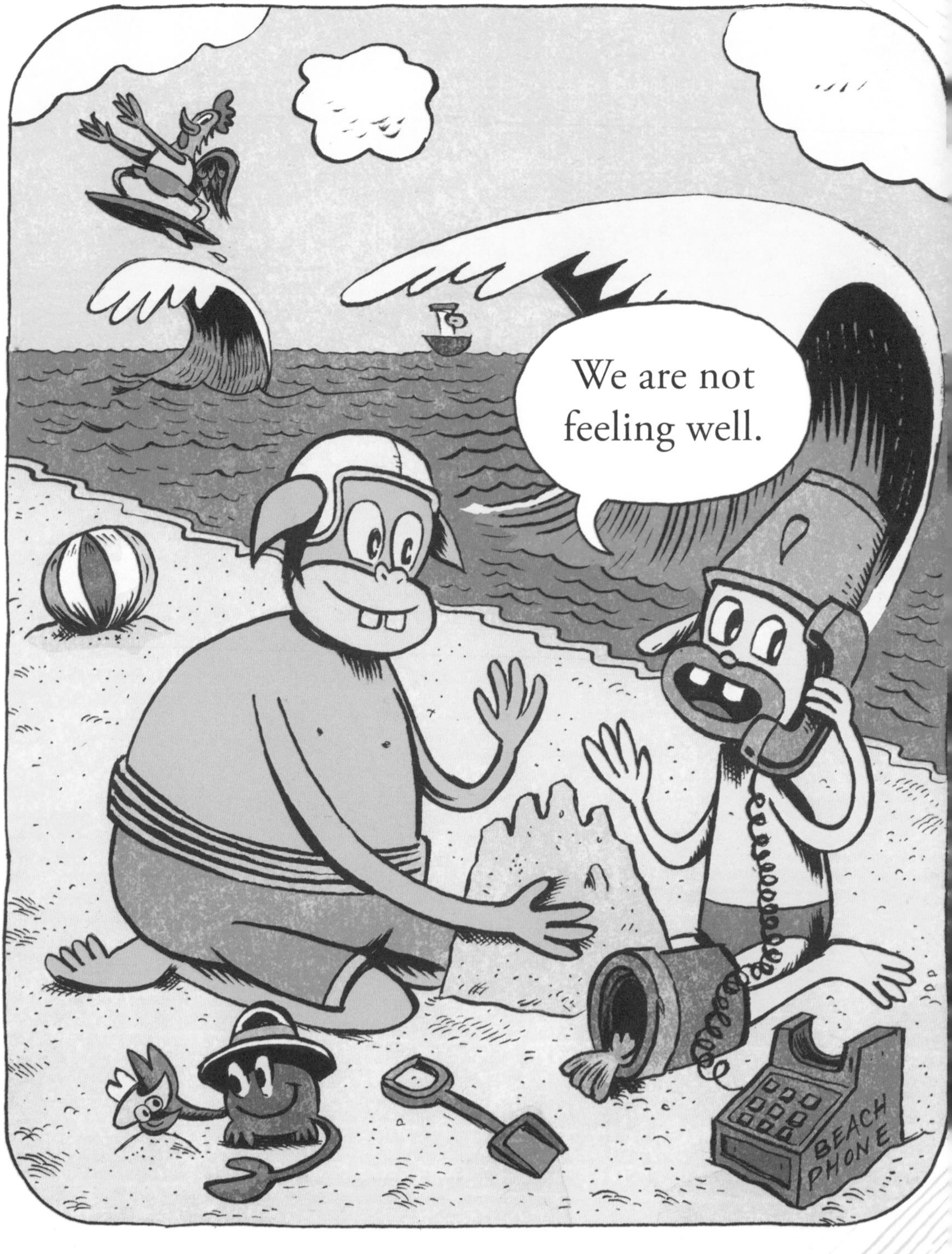
We are not feeling well.
BEACH PHONE

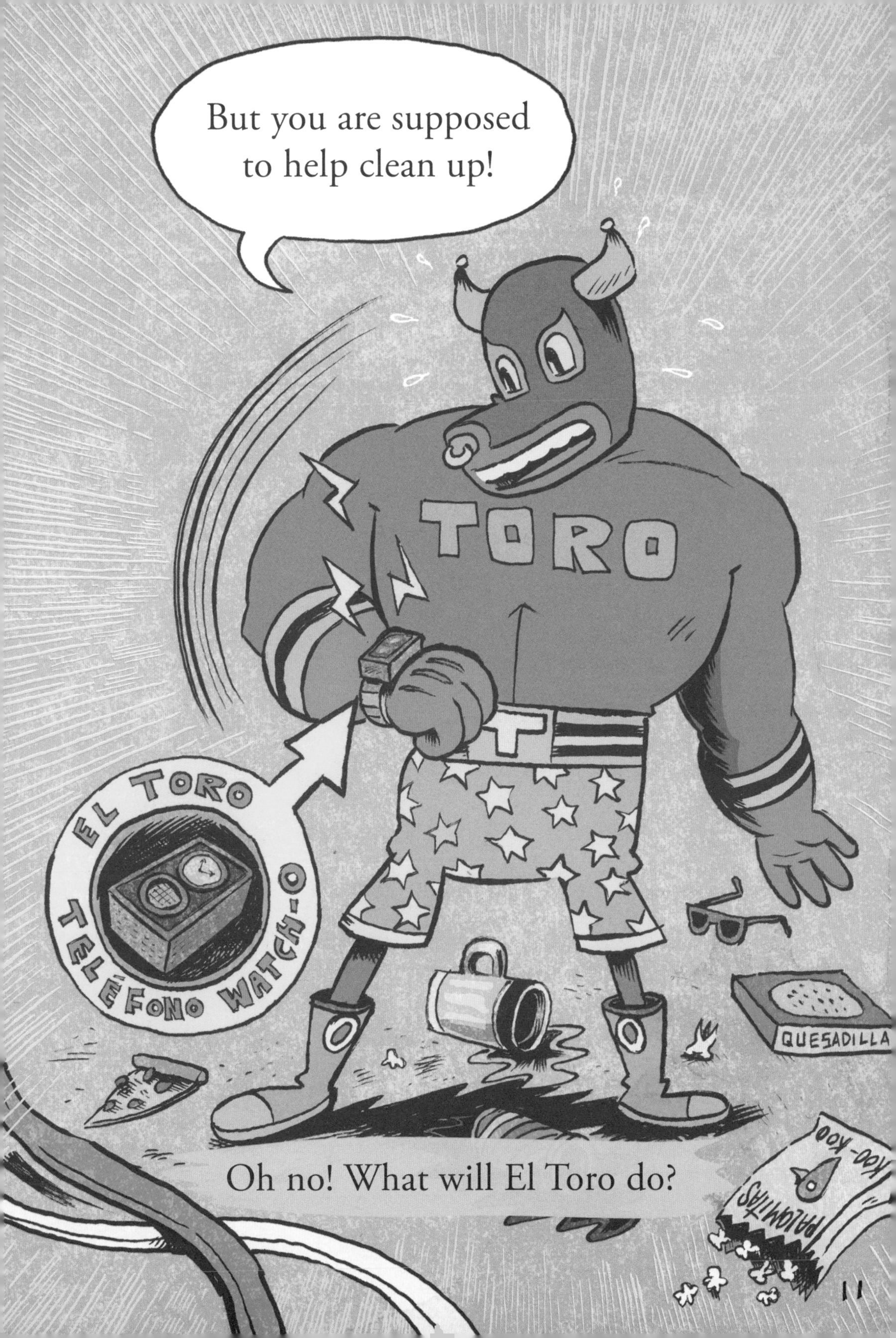
But you are supposed to help clean up!
TORO
T
EL TORO
TELÉFONO WATCH-O
QUESADILLA
koo-koo
PALOMITAS
Oh no! What will El Toro do?

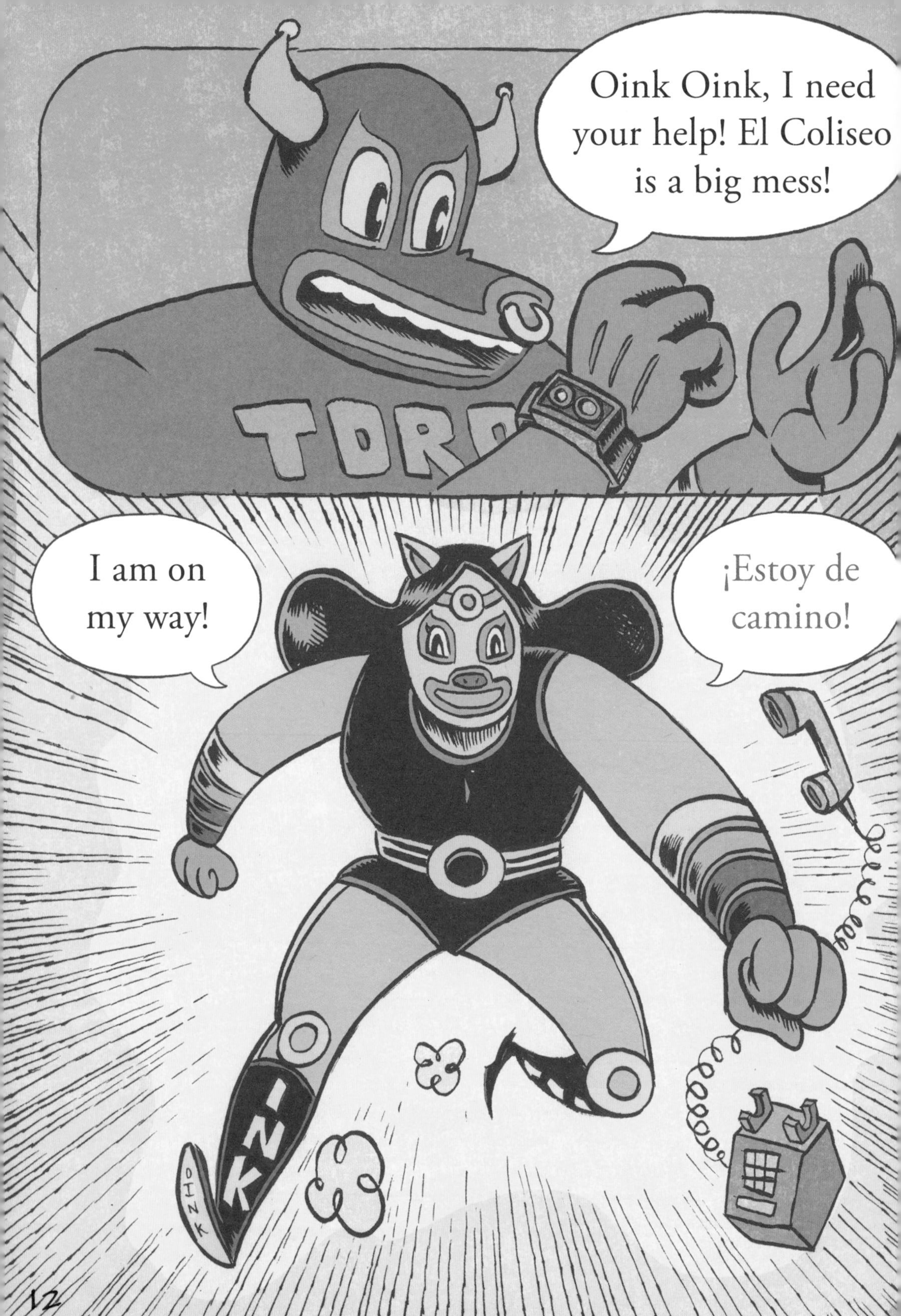
Oink Oink, I need your help! El Coliseo is a big mess!
I am on my way!
¡Estoy de camino!
INK
OINK

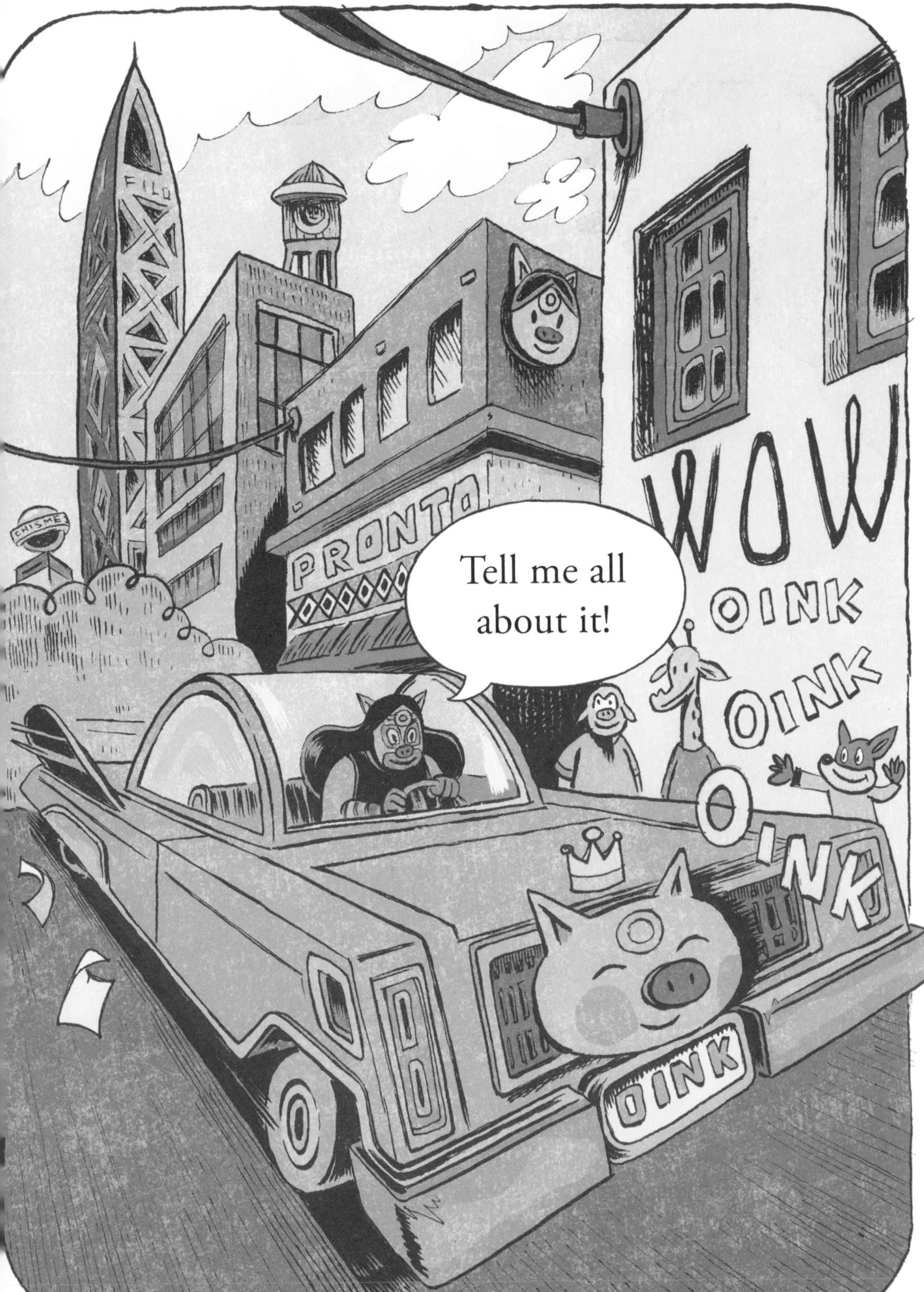
FILO
CHISME
PRONTO
Tell me all about it!
WOW
OINK
OINK
OINK
OINK

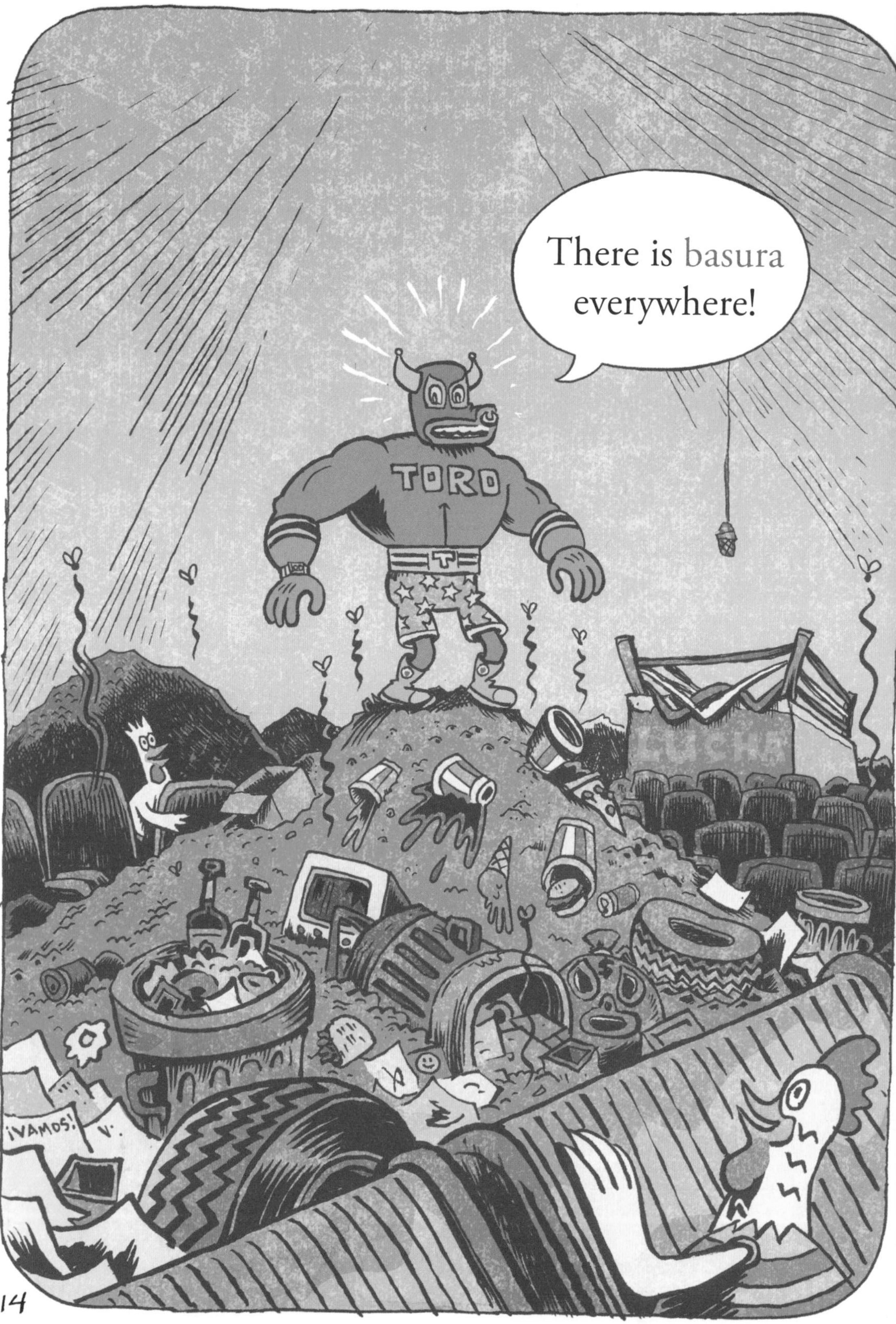
There is basura everywhere!
TORO
¡VAMOS!

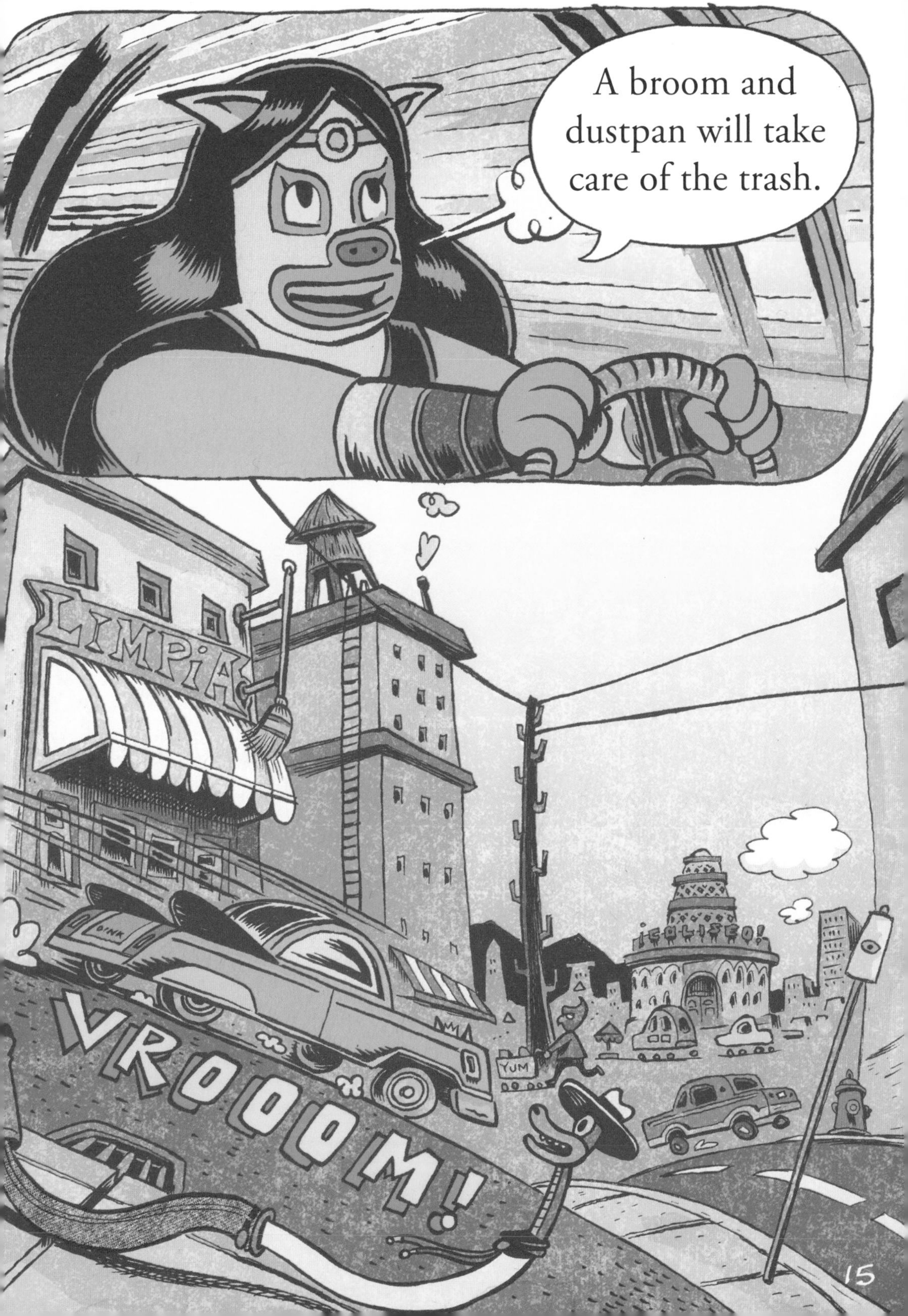
A broom and dustpan will take care of the trash.
LIMPIA
¡COLISEO!
YUM
VROOOOM!

The floors are sticky!

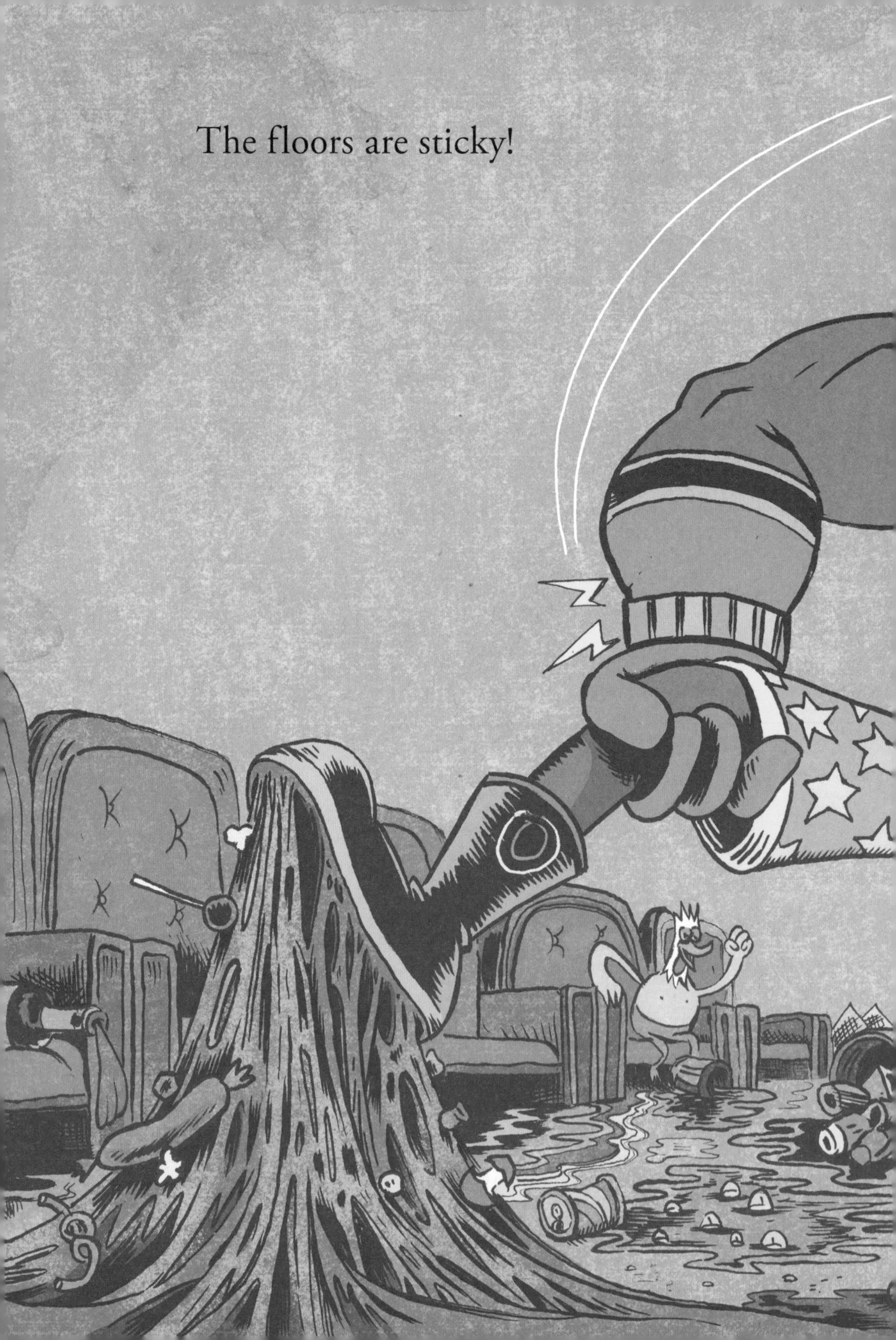

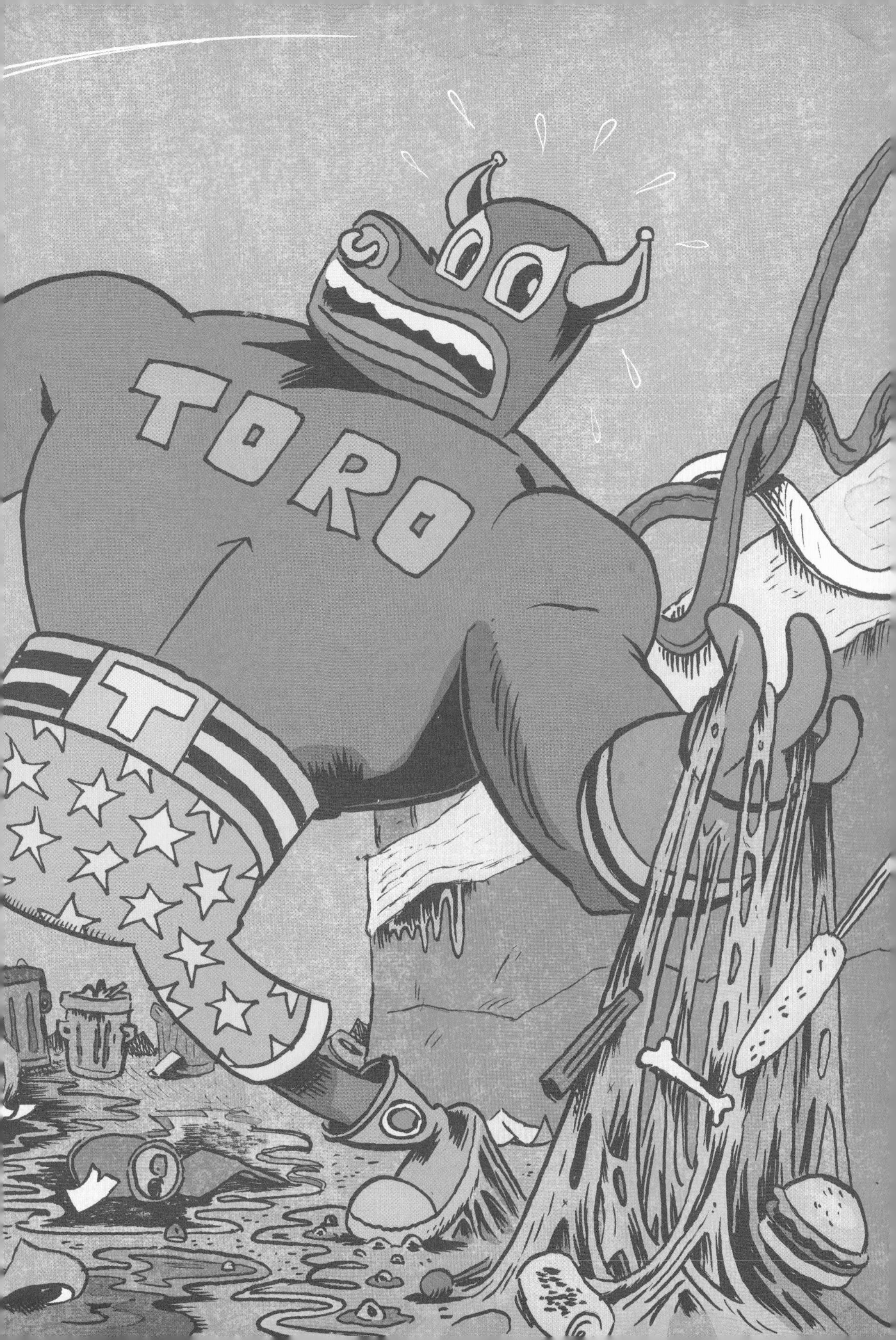
TORO
T

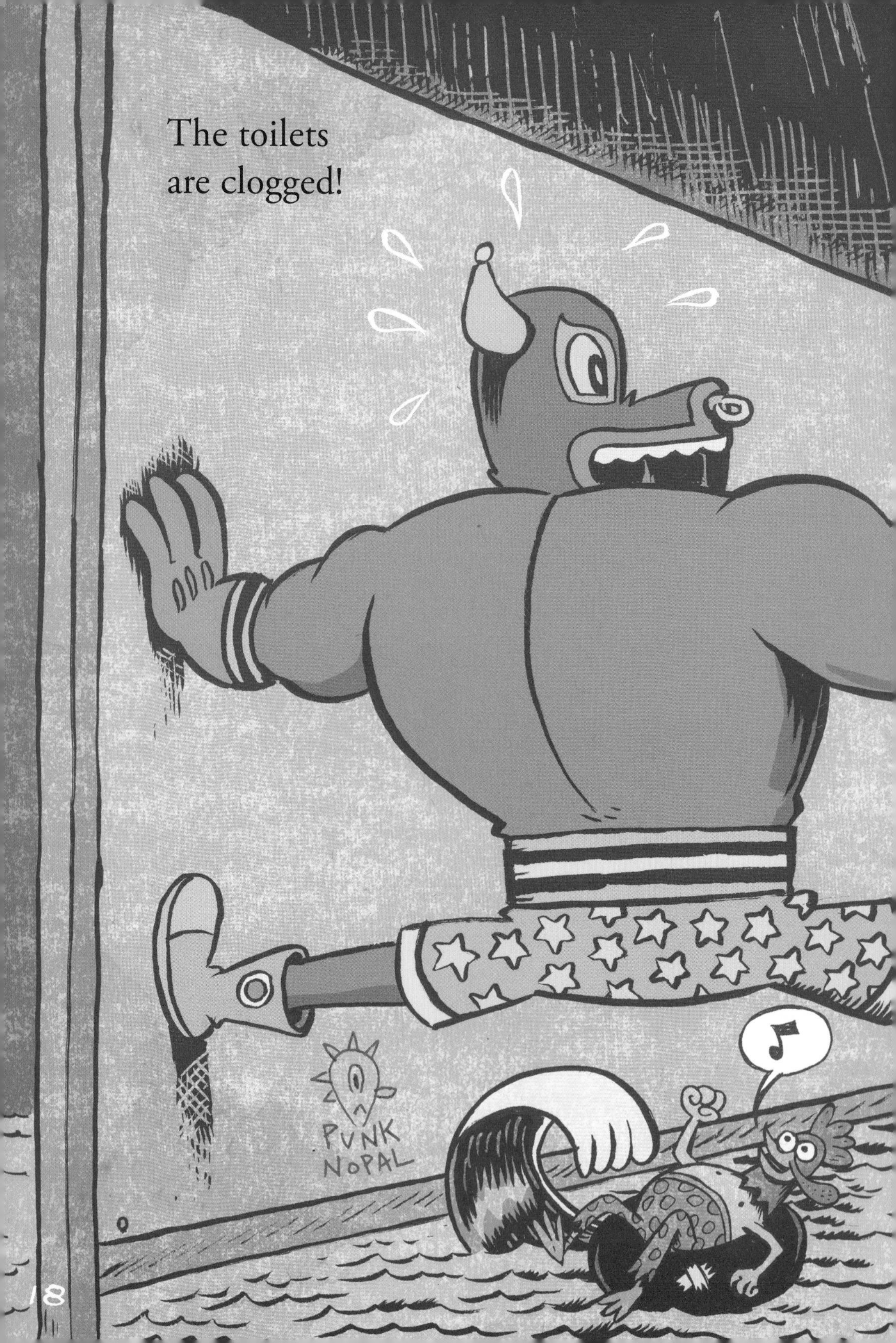
The toilets
are clogged!
PUNK
NOPAL

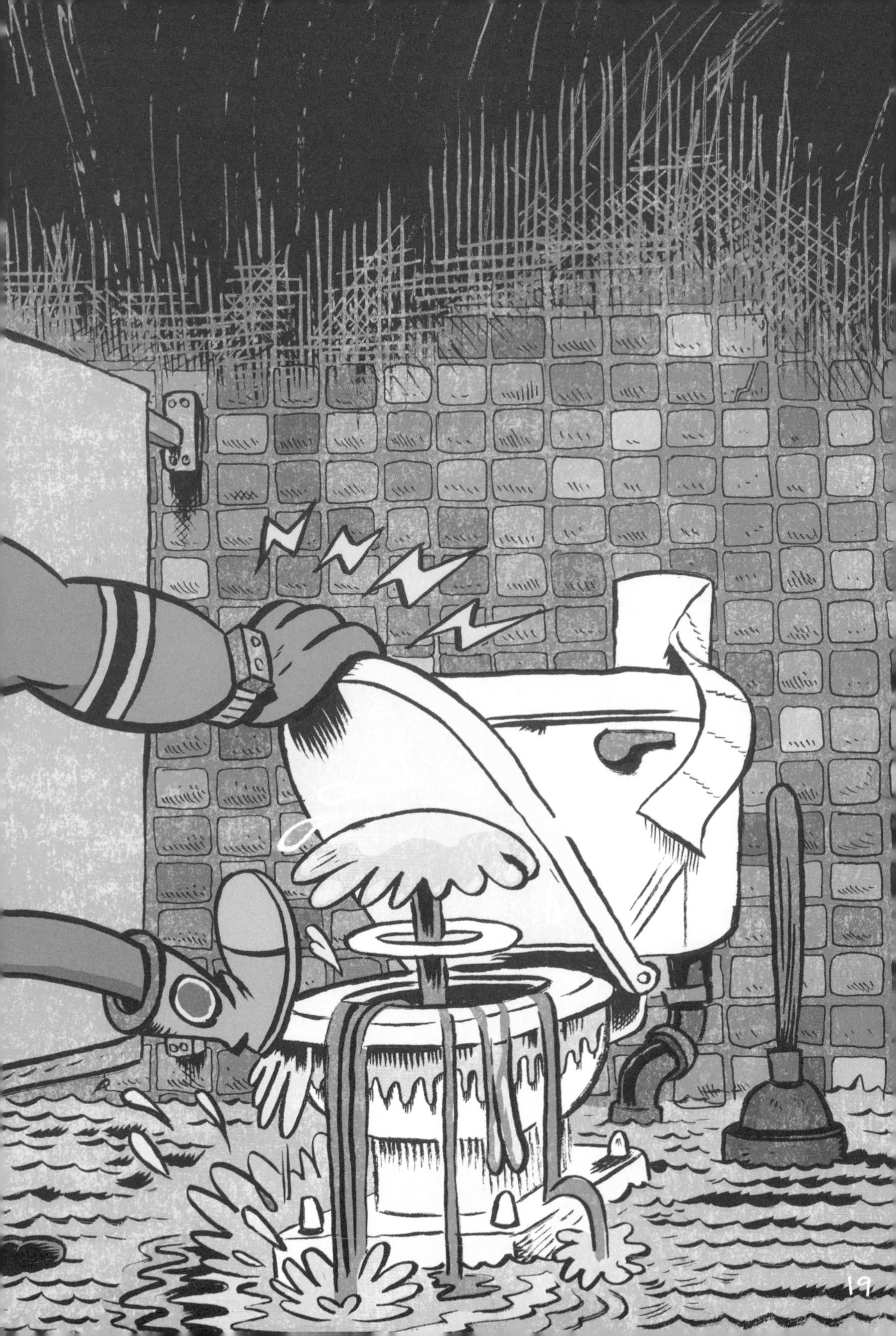

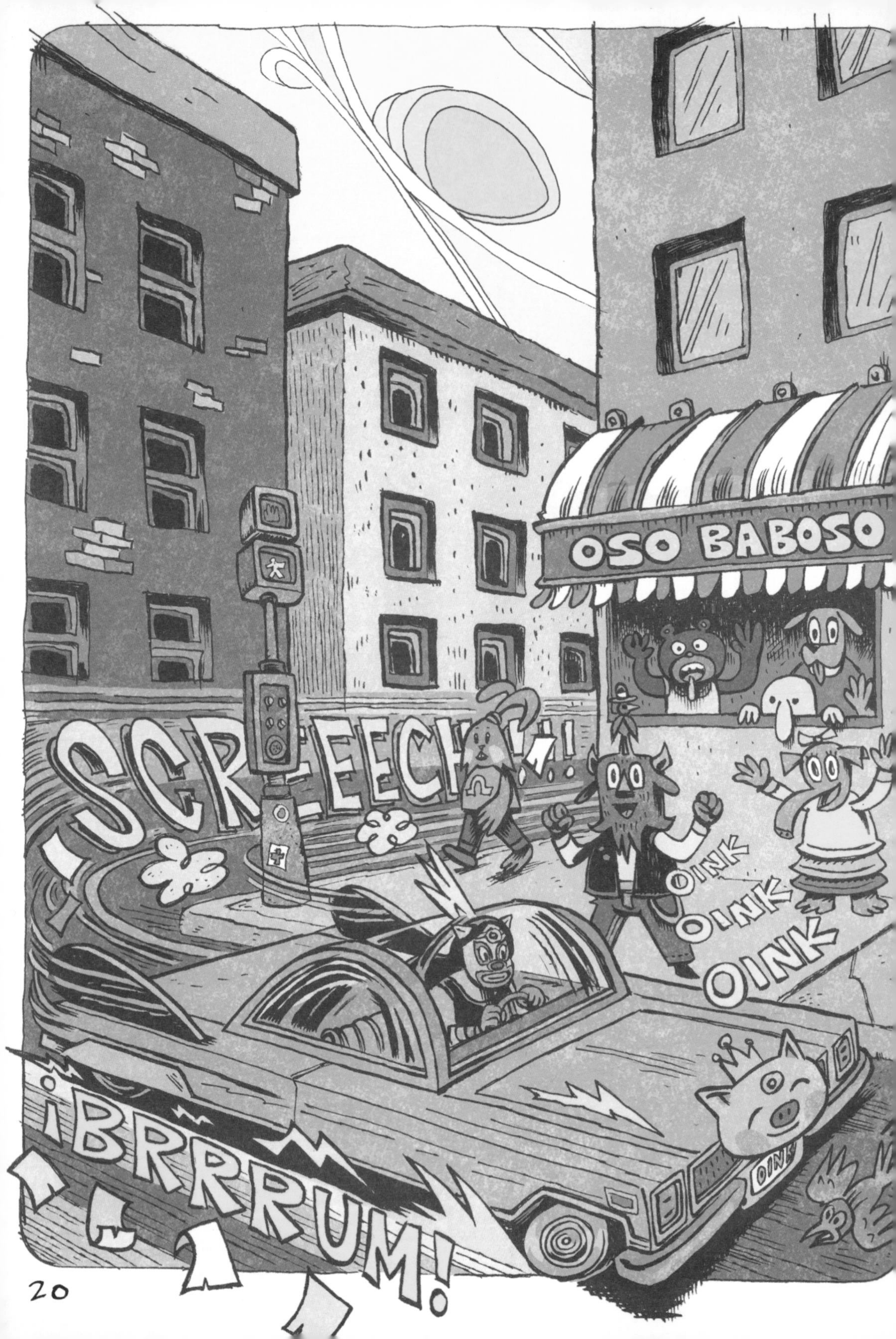
OSO BABOSO
SCREECH
OINK
OINK
OINK
OINK
¡BRRRRUM!

The sink is full of dirty dishes!

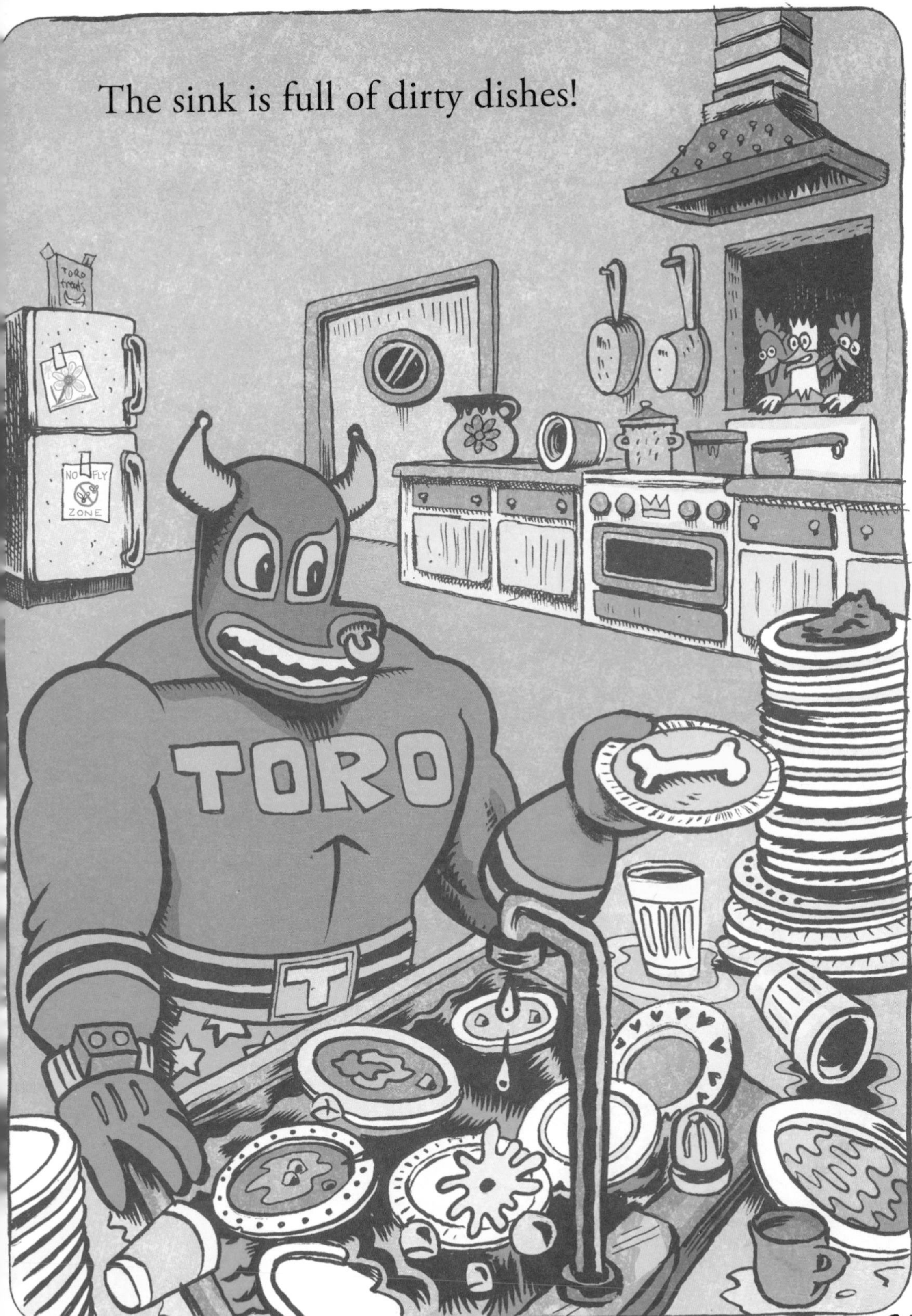
NO FLY ZONE
TORO
T

And to top it all off, the training chickens got loose.

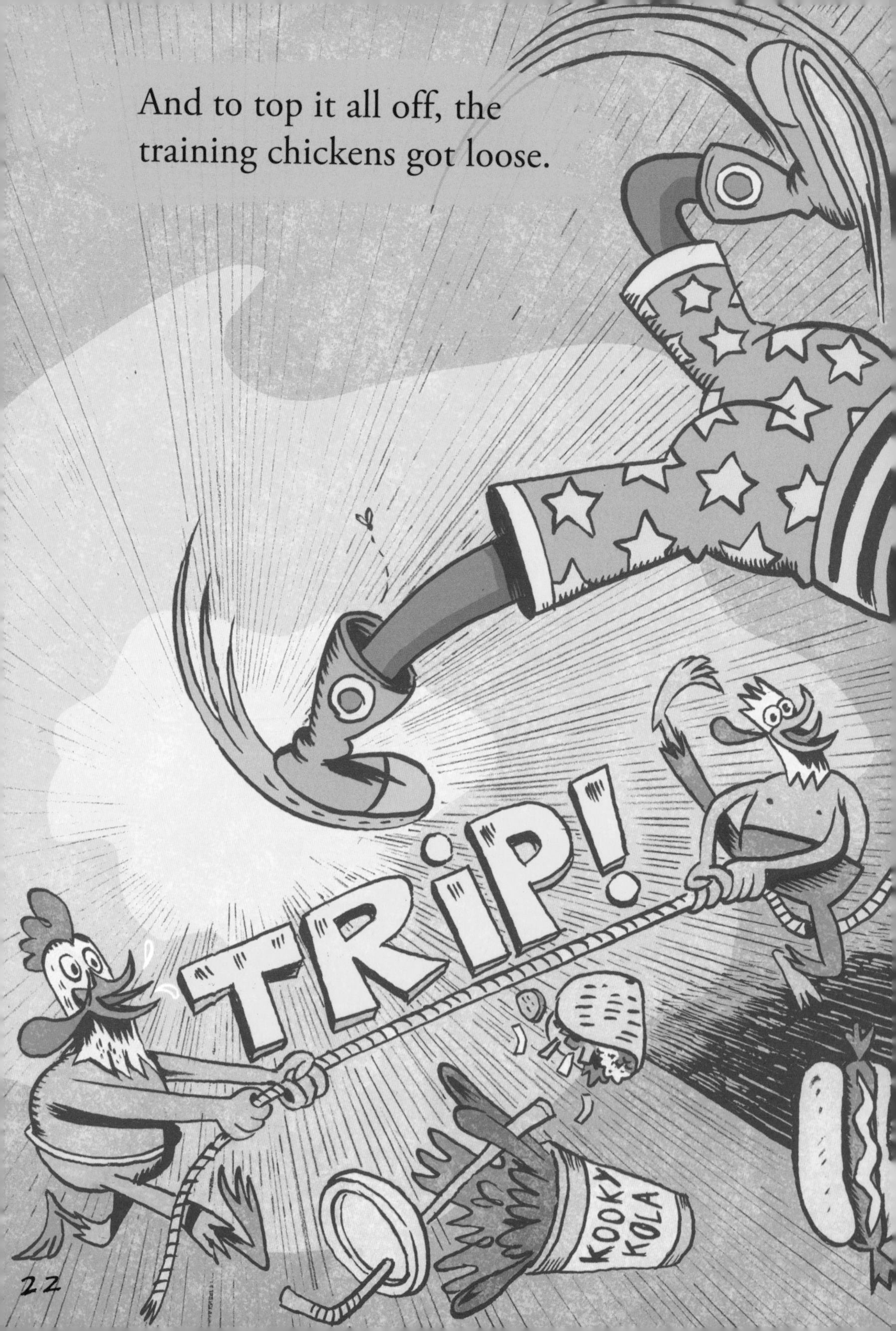
TRIP!
KOOKY KOLA

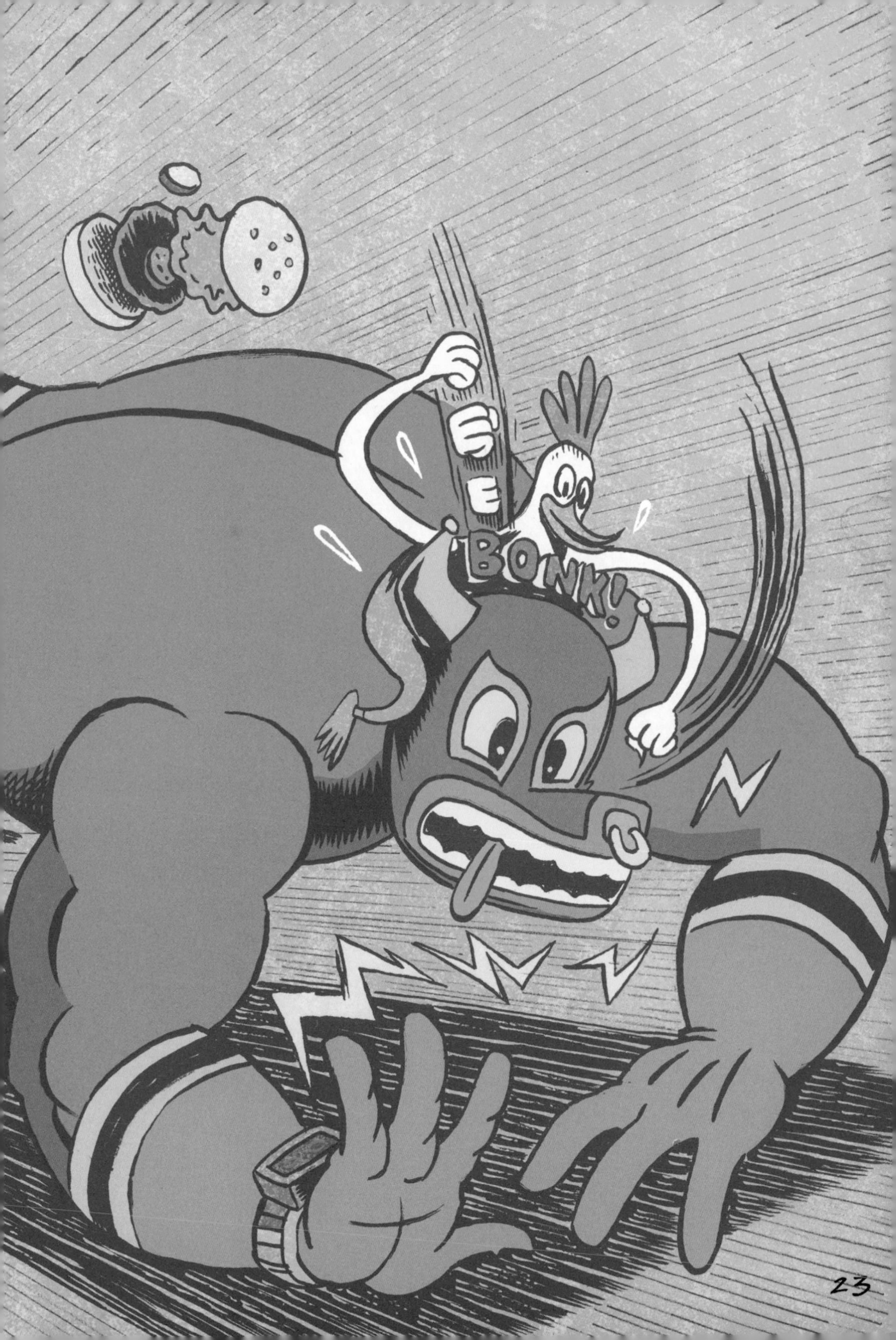
BONK!

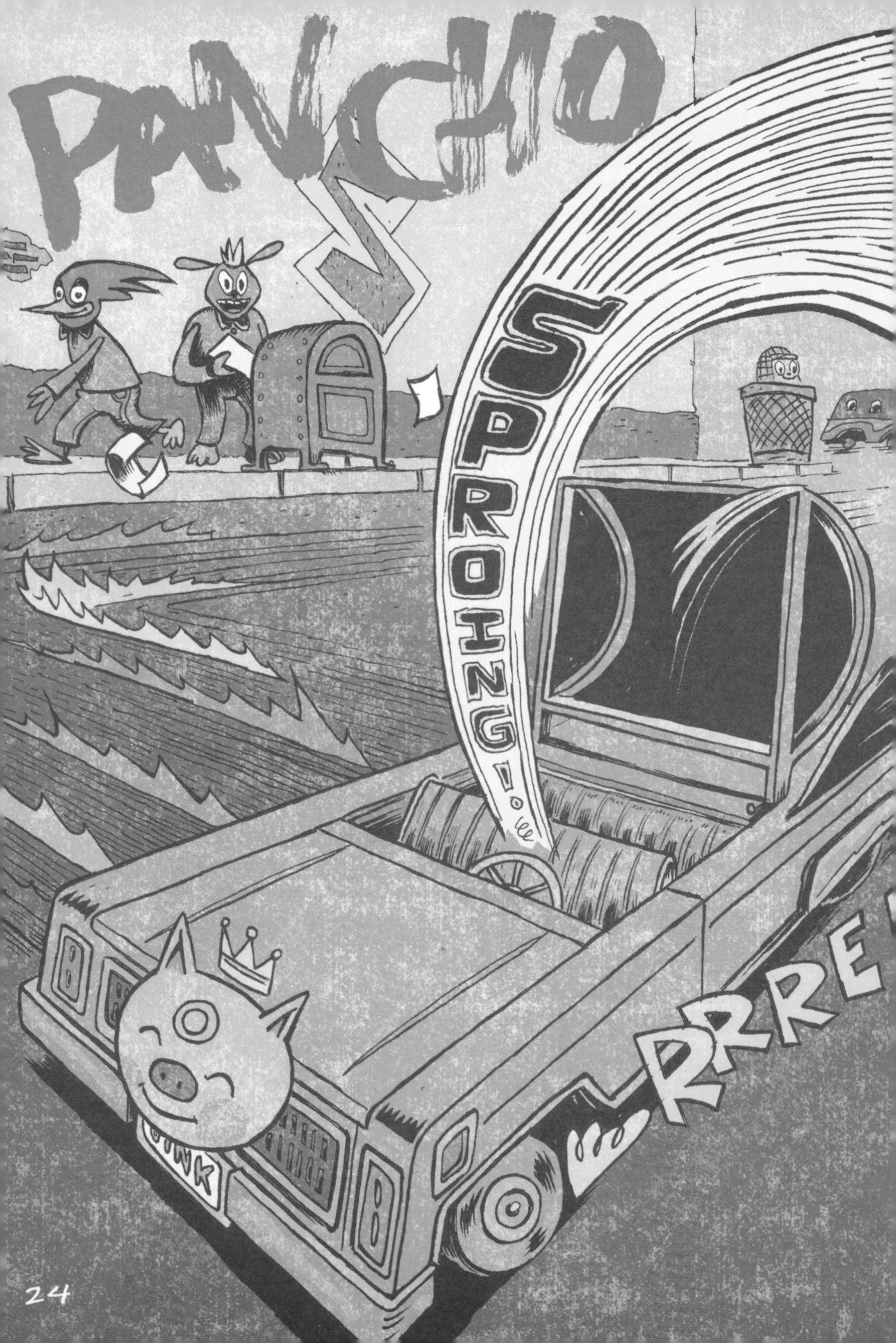
PANCHO
SPROING!
OINK
RRRE

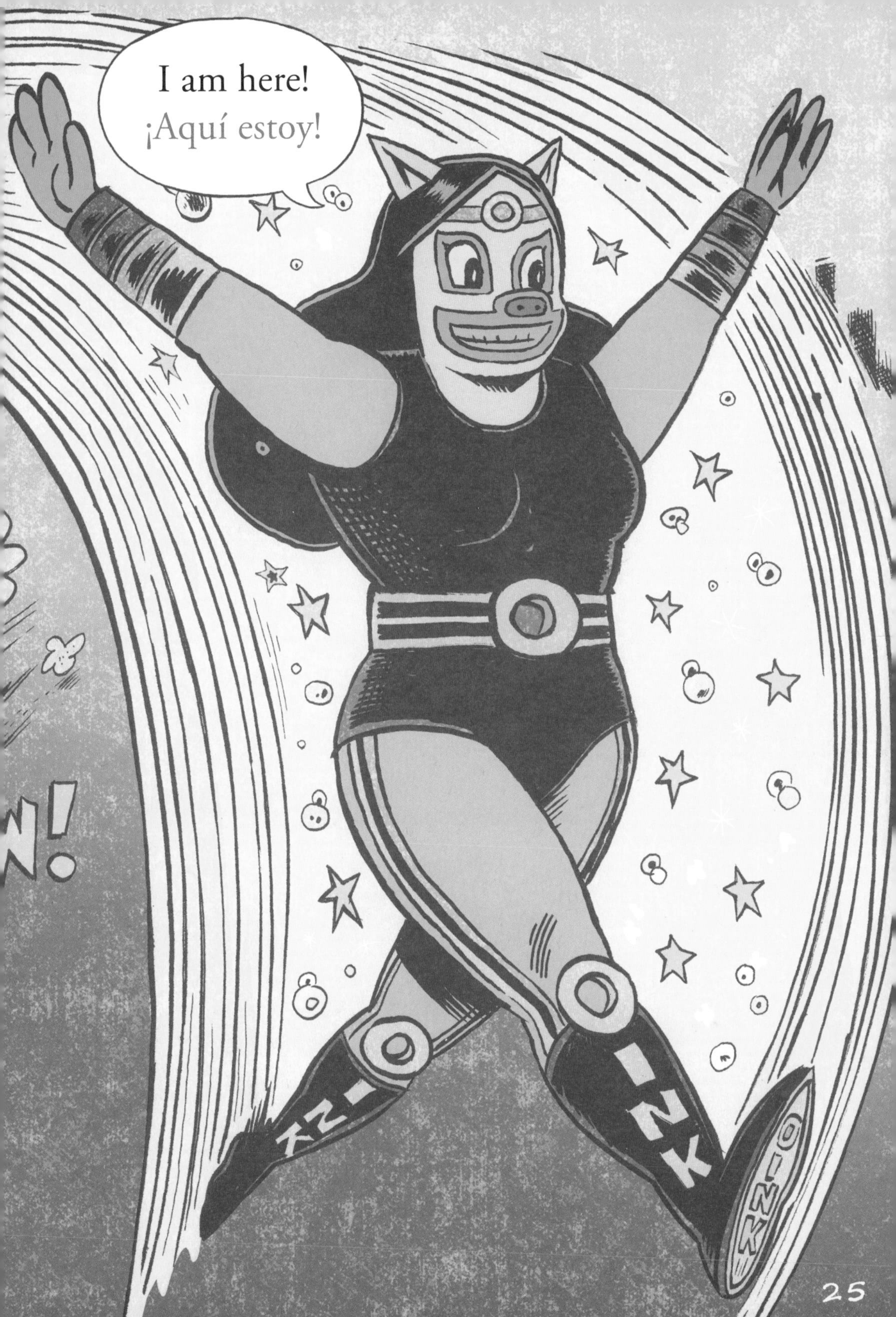
I am here!
¡Aquí estoy!
OINK

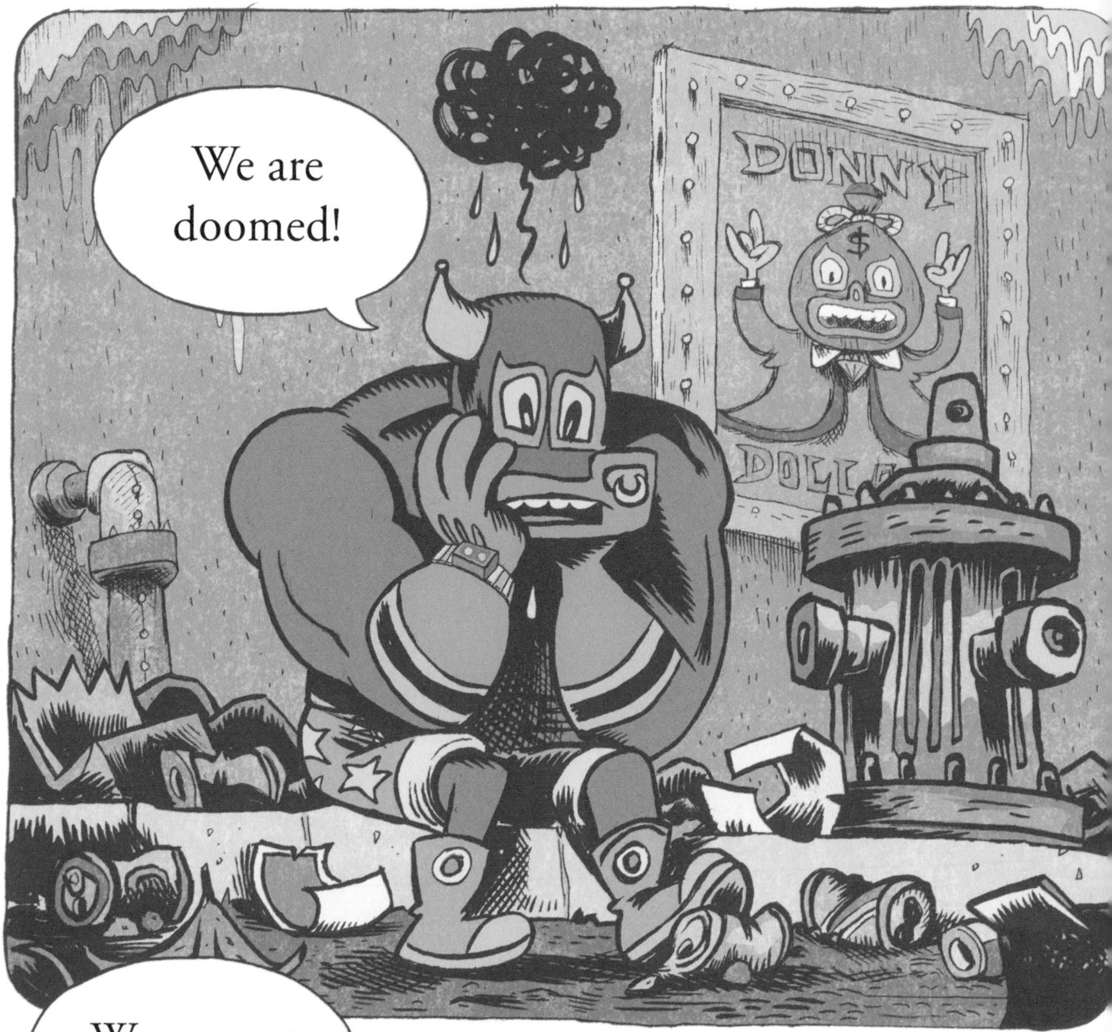
We are doomed!
DONNY

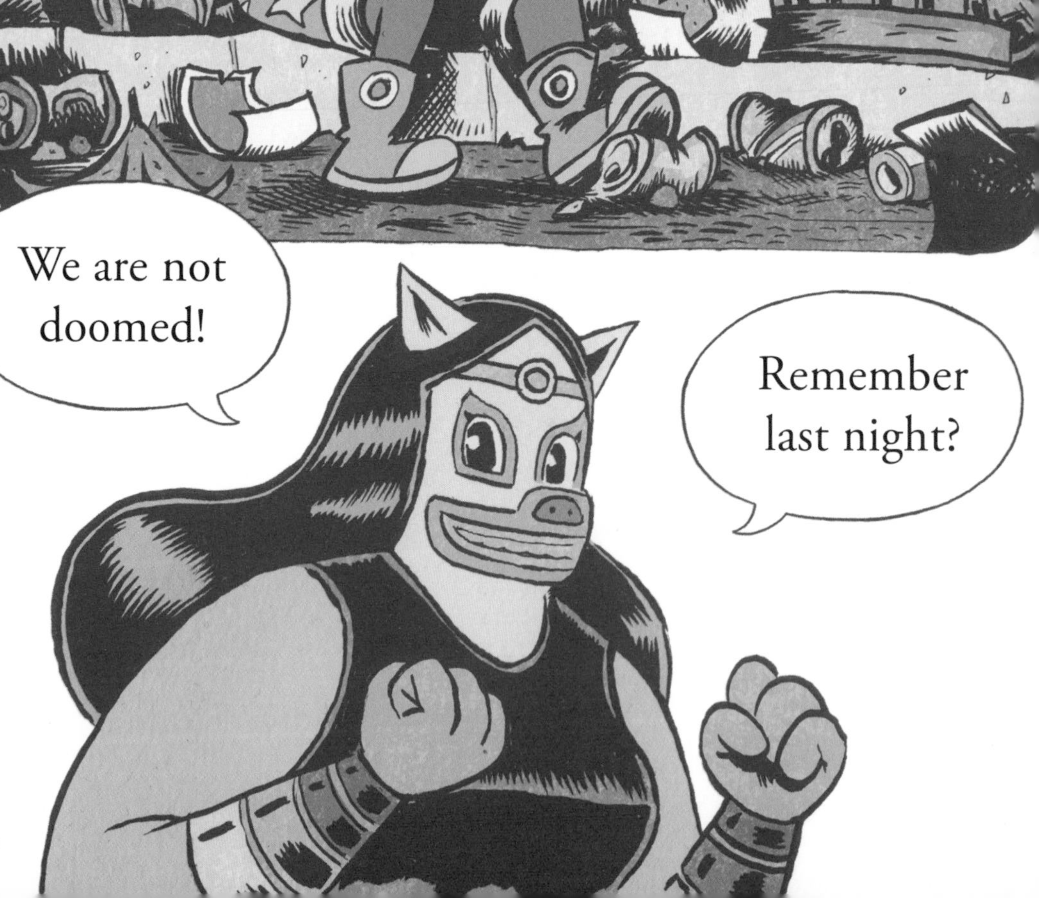
We are not doomed!
Remember last night?

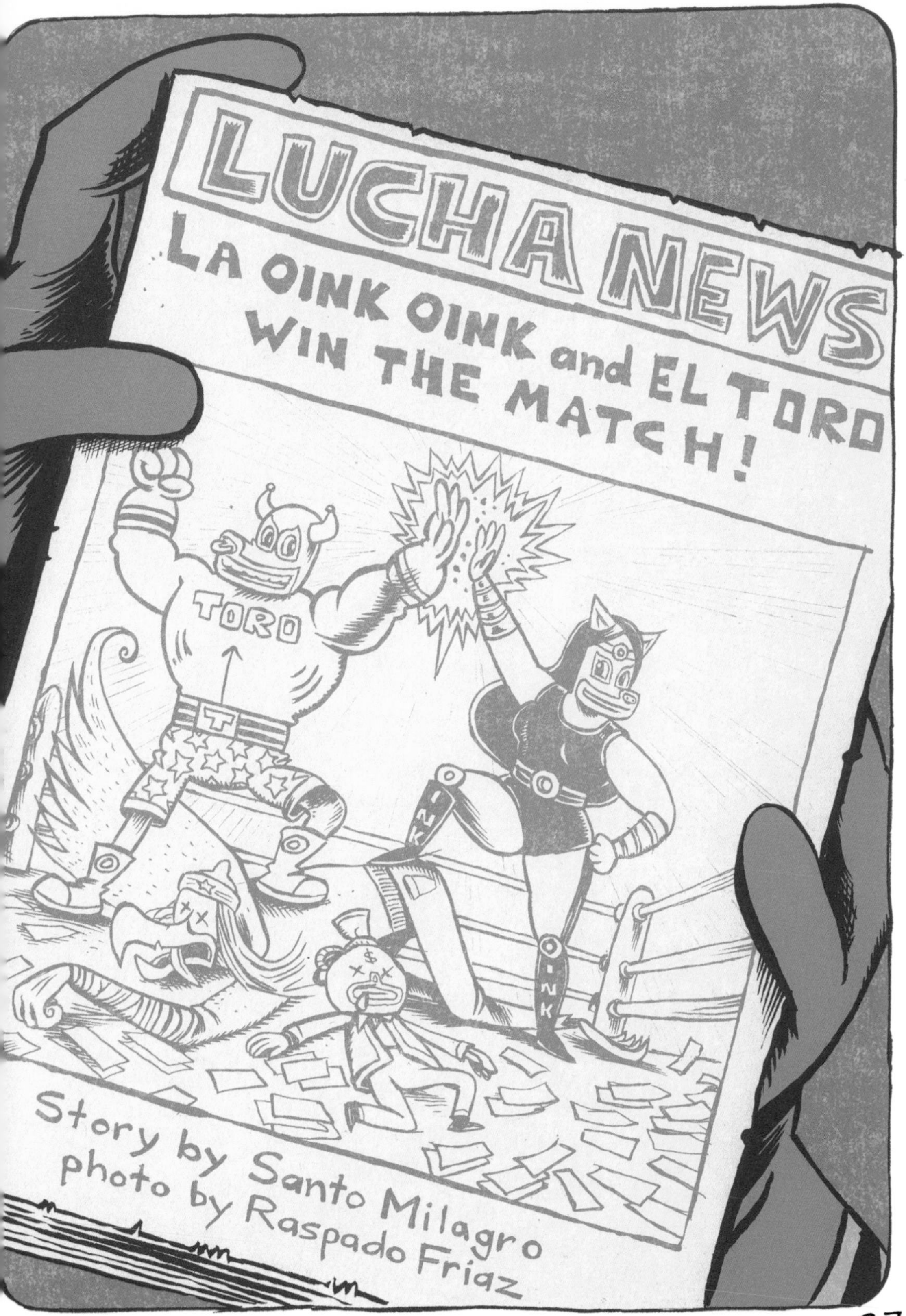
LUCHA NEWS
LA OINK OINK and EL TORO WIN THE MATCH!
TORO
T
OINK
OINK
$
Story by Santo Milagro
photo by Raspado Friaz

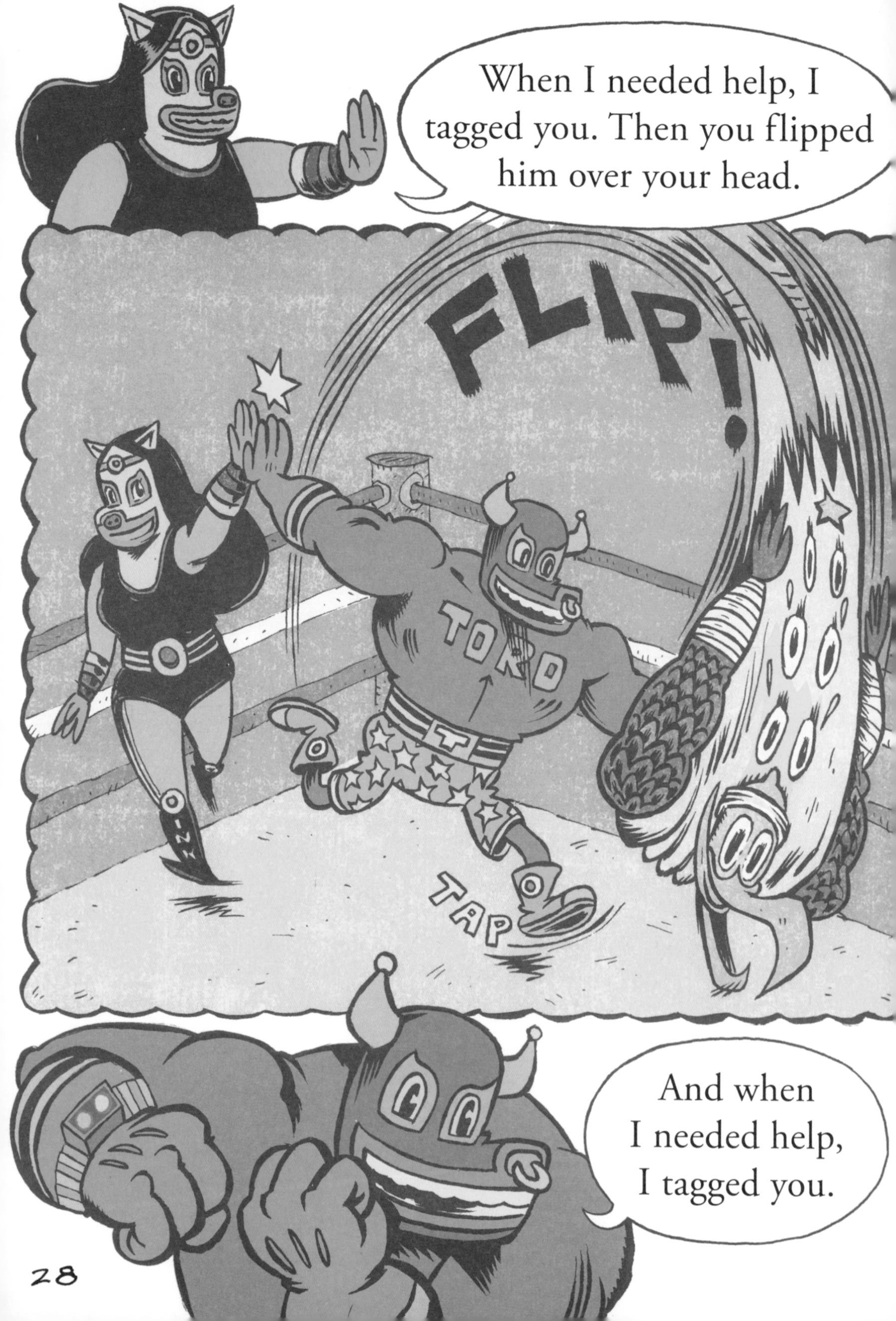
When I needed help, I tagged you. Then you flipped him over your head.
FLIP!
TORO
TAP
And when I needed help, I tagged you.

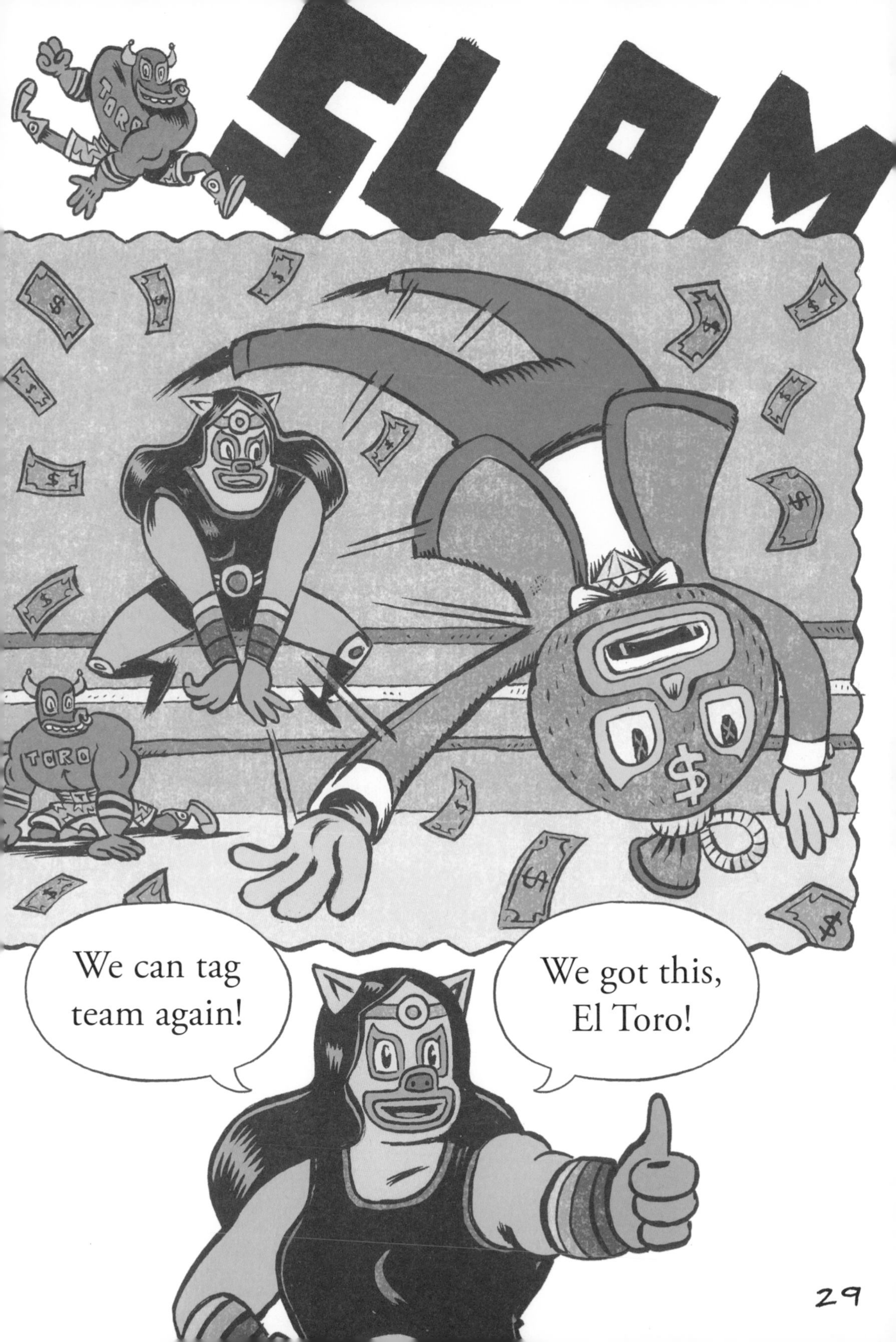
SLAM
TORO
TORO
We can tag team again!
We got this, El Toro!

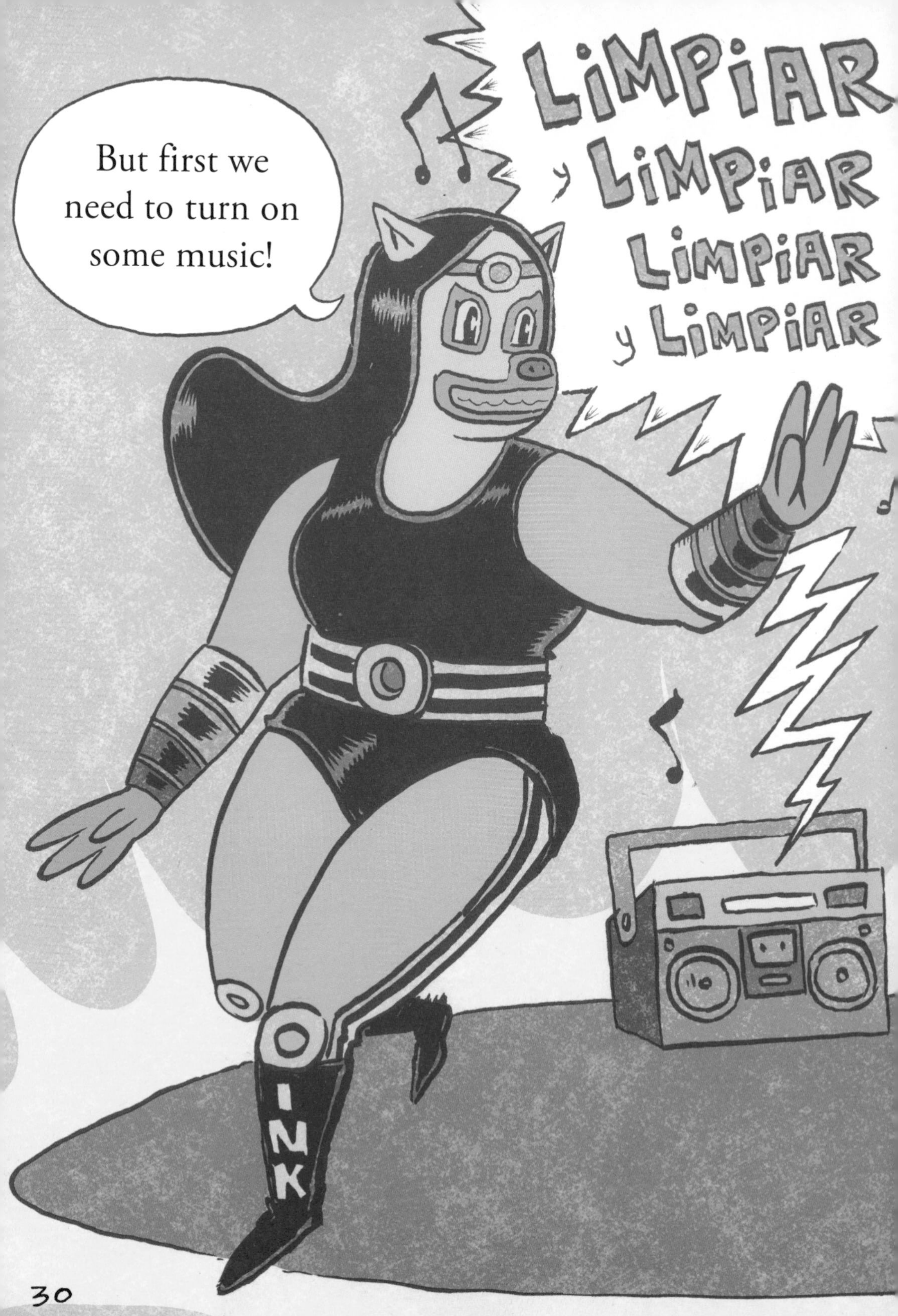
But first we need to turn on some music!
LiMPiAR
y LiMPiAR
LiMPiAR
y LiMPiAR
INK

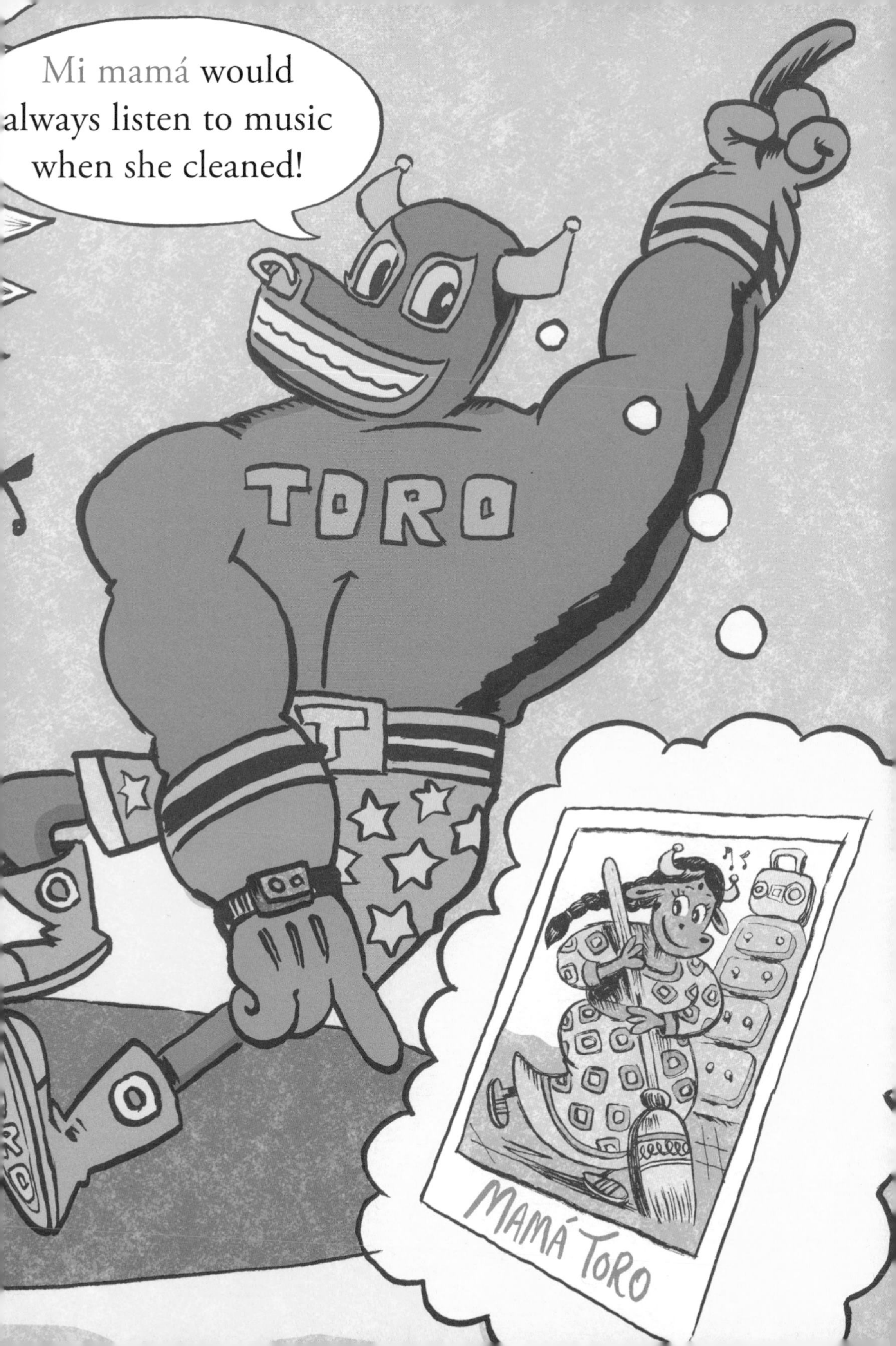
Mi mamá would always listen to music when she cleaned!
TORO
MAMÁ TORO

La Oink Oink grabs la escoba and dances around the room.

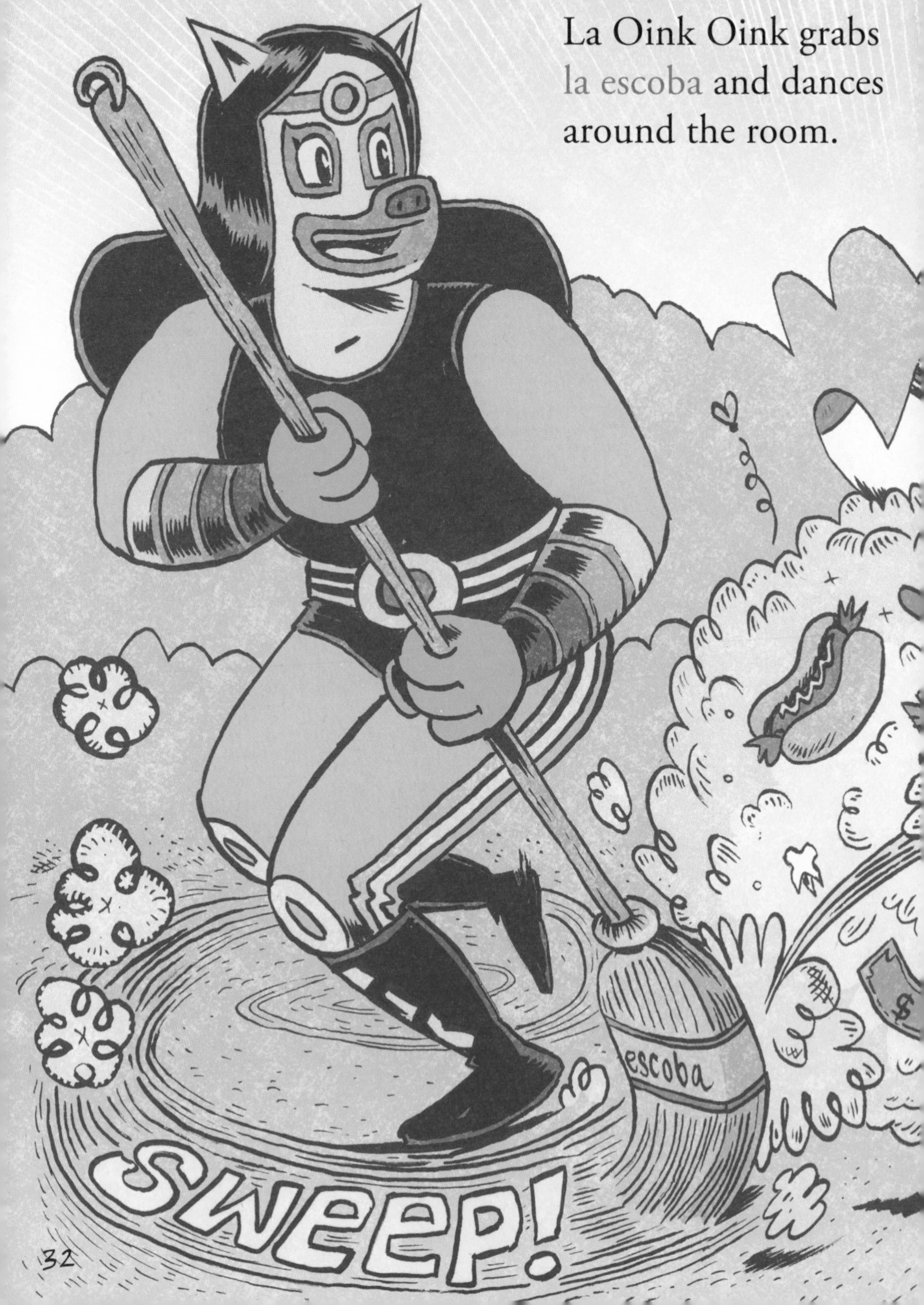
escoba
SWEEP!

El Toro uses the dustpan
to gather up the trash.

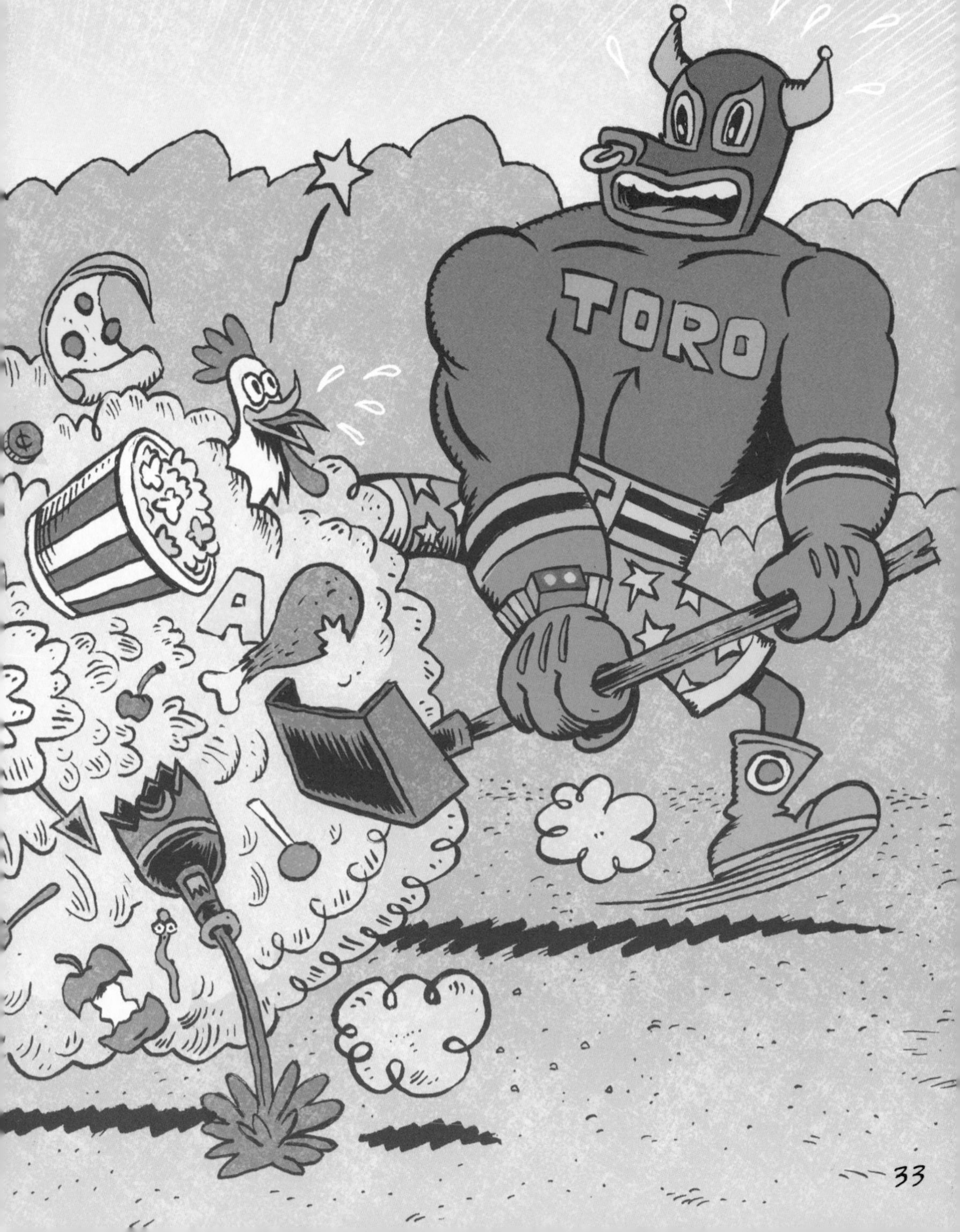

TORO

El Toro mops

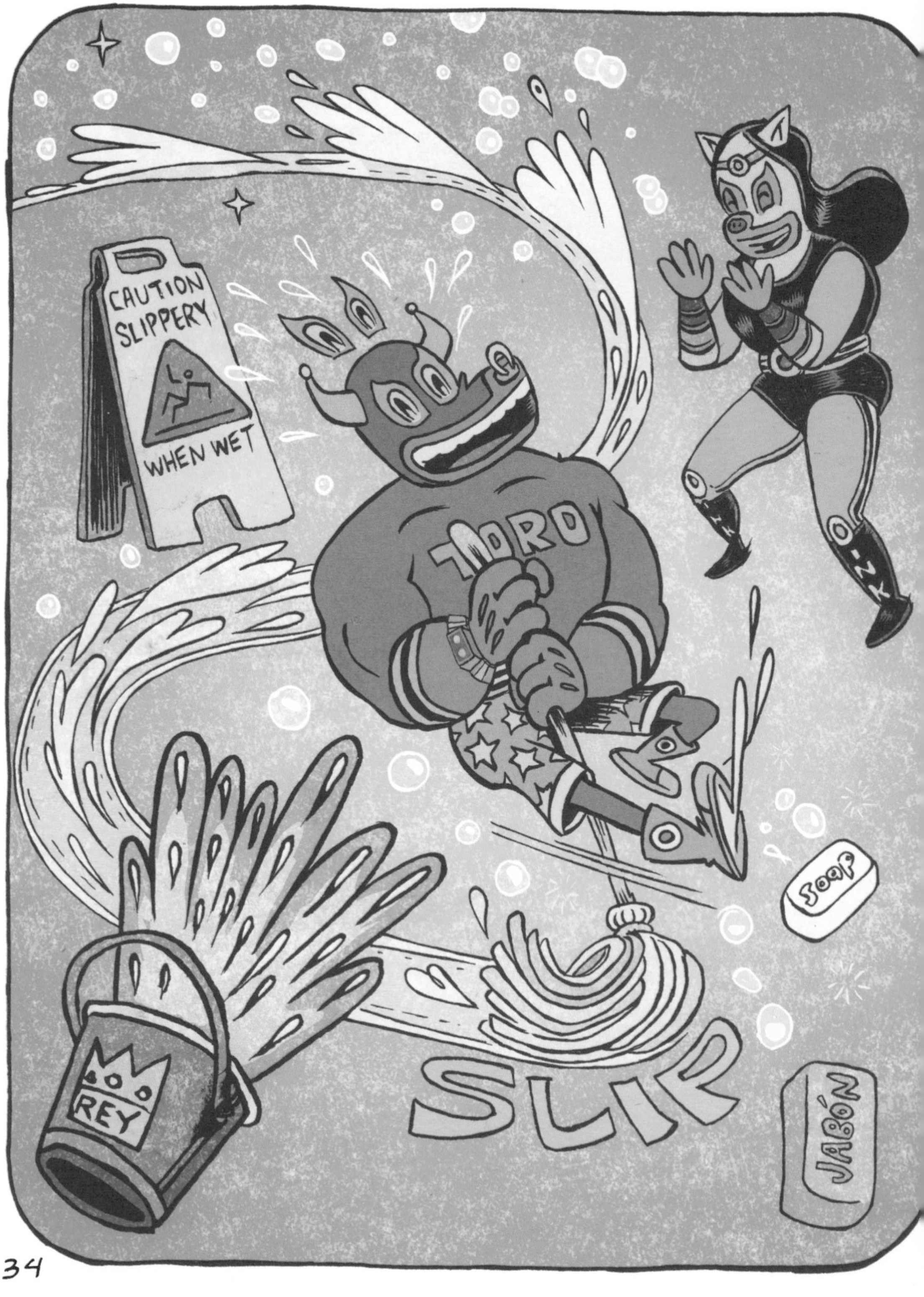
CAUTION
SLIPPERY
WHEN WET
TORO
REY
SLIP
SOAP
JABÓN

and La Oink Oink blows the floor dry.

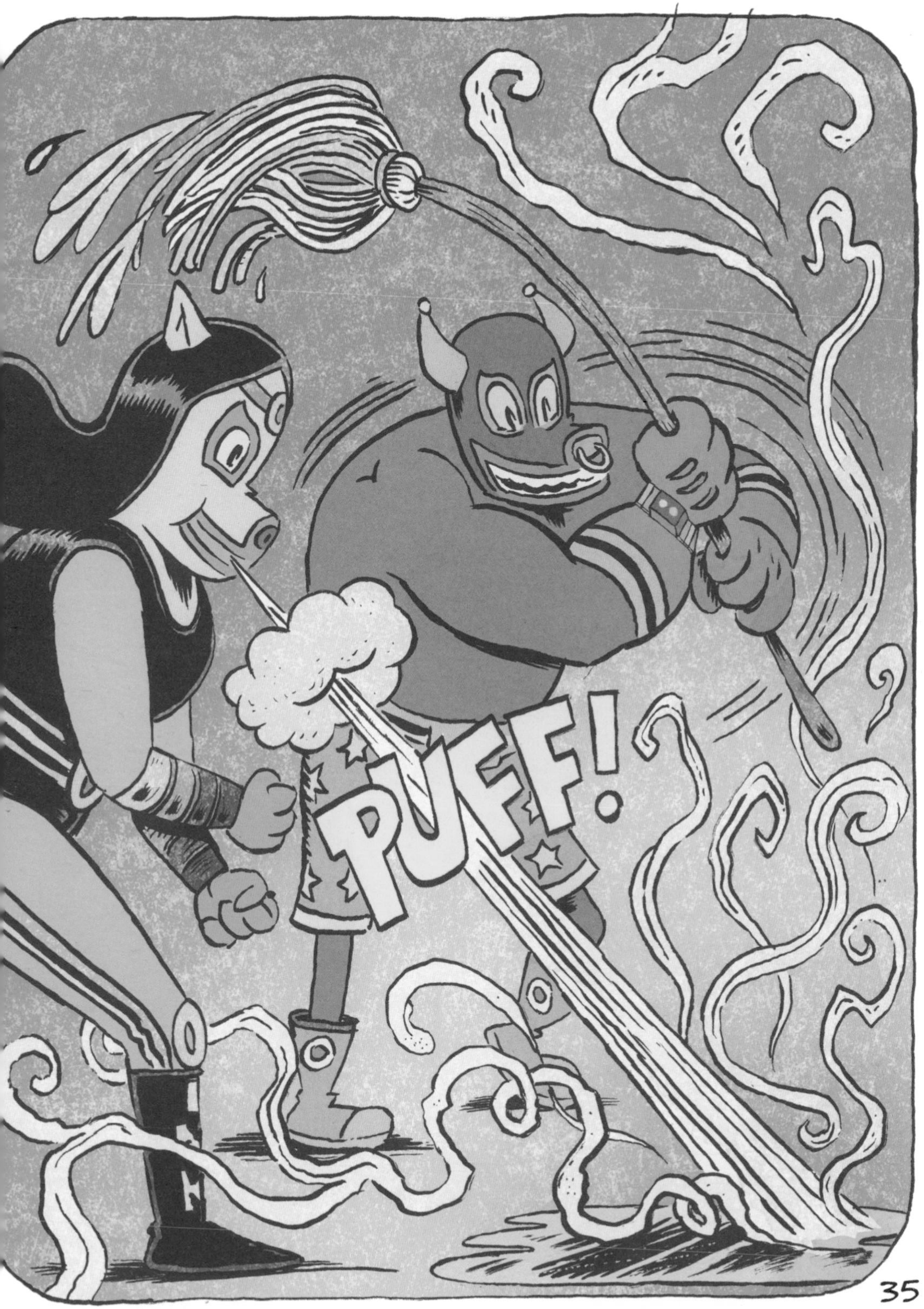
PUFF!

La Oink Oink
battles the toilets.

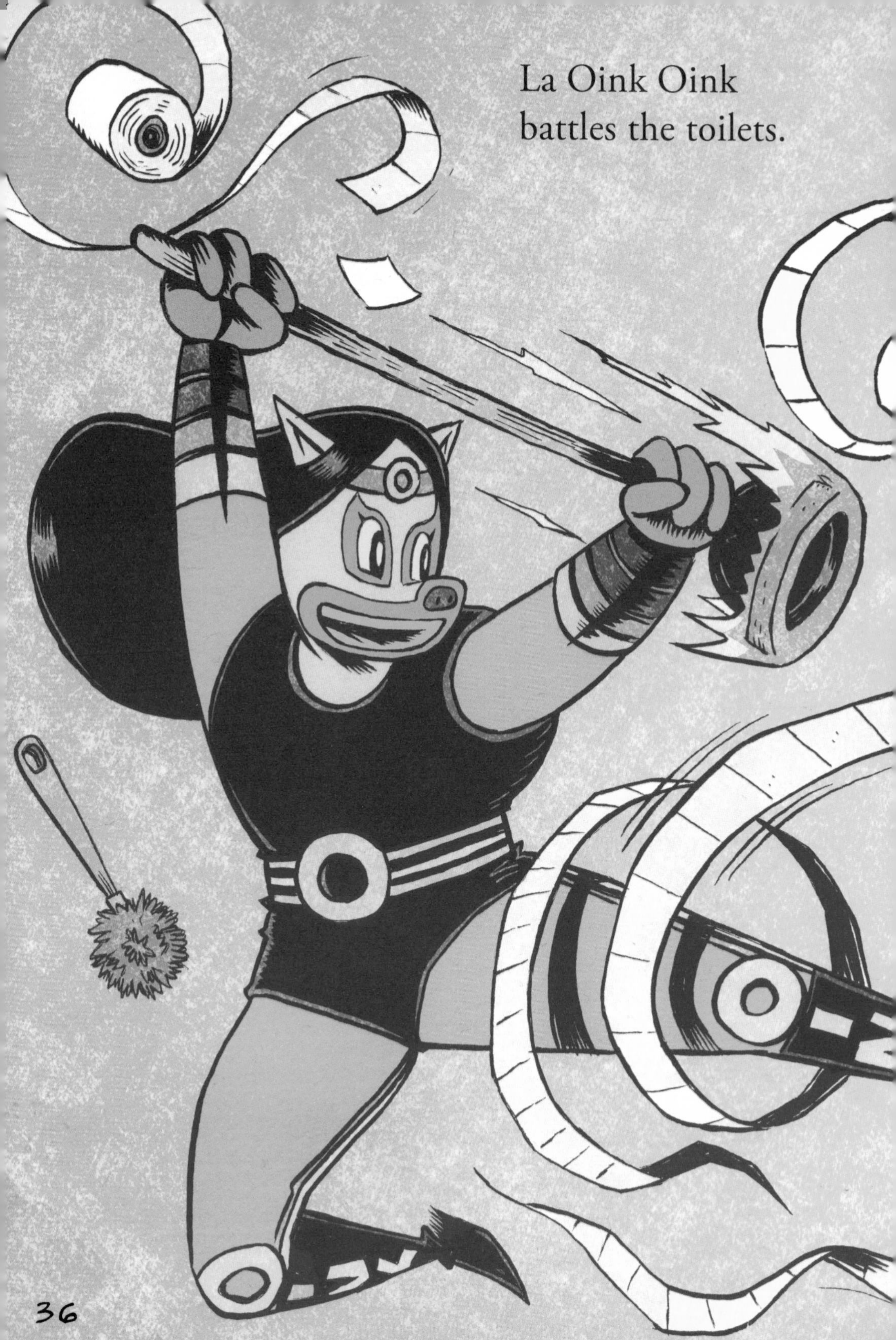

El Toro holds
his nose and jiggles
the handle.

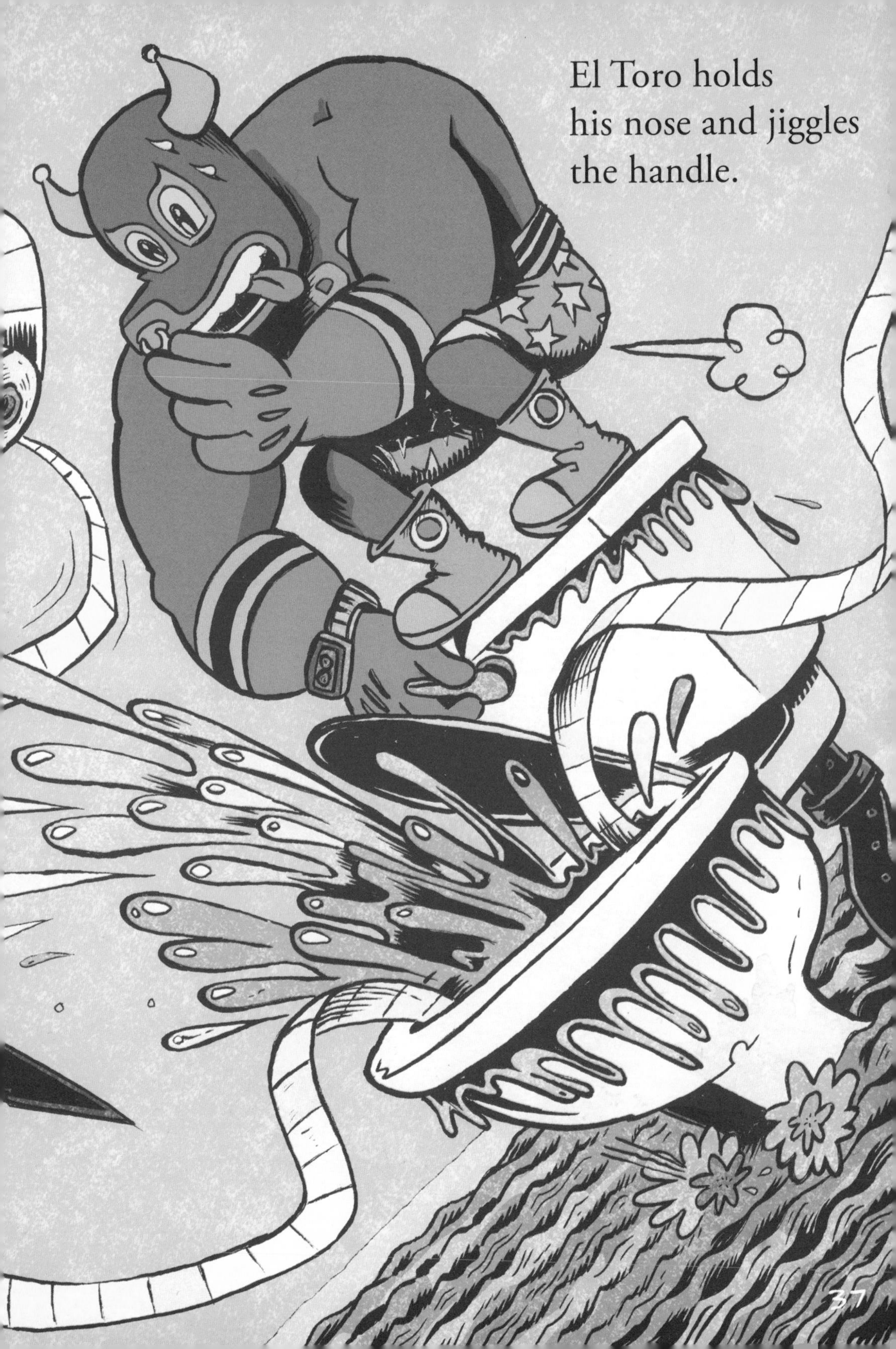

El Toro stretches the canvas and
La Oink Oink tightens the ropes!

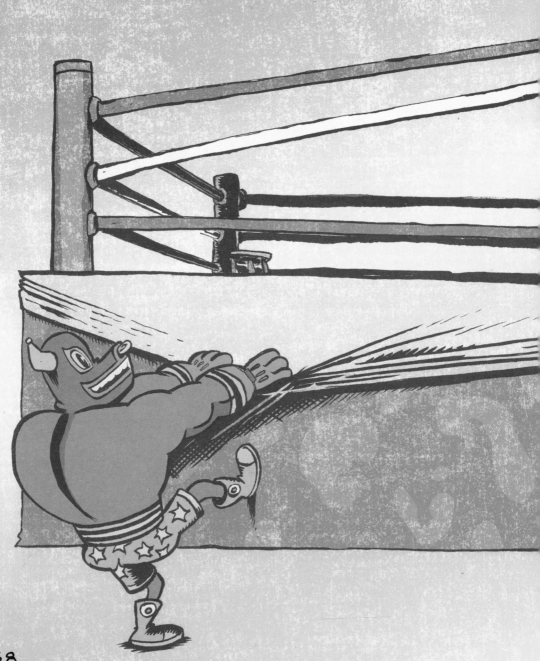

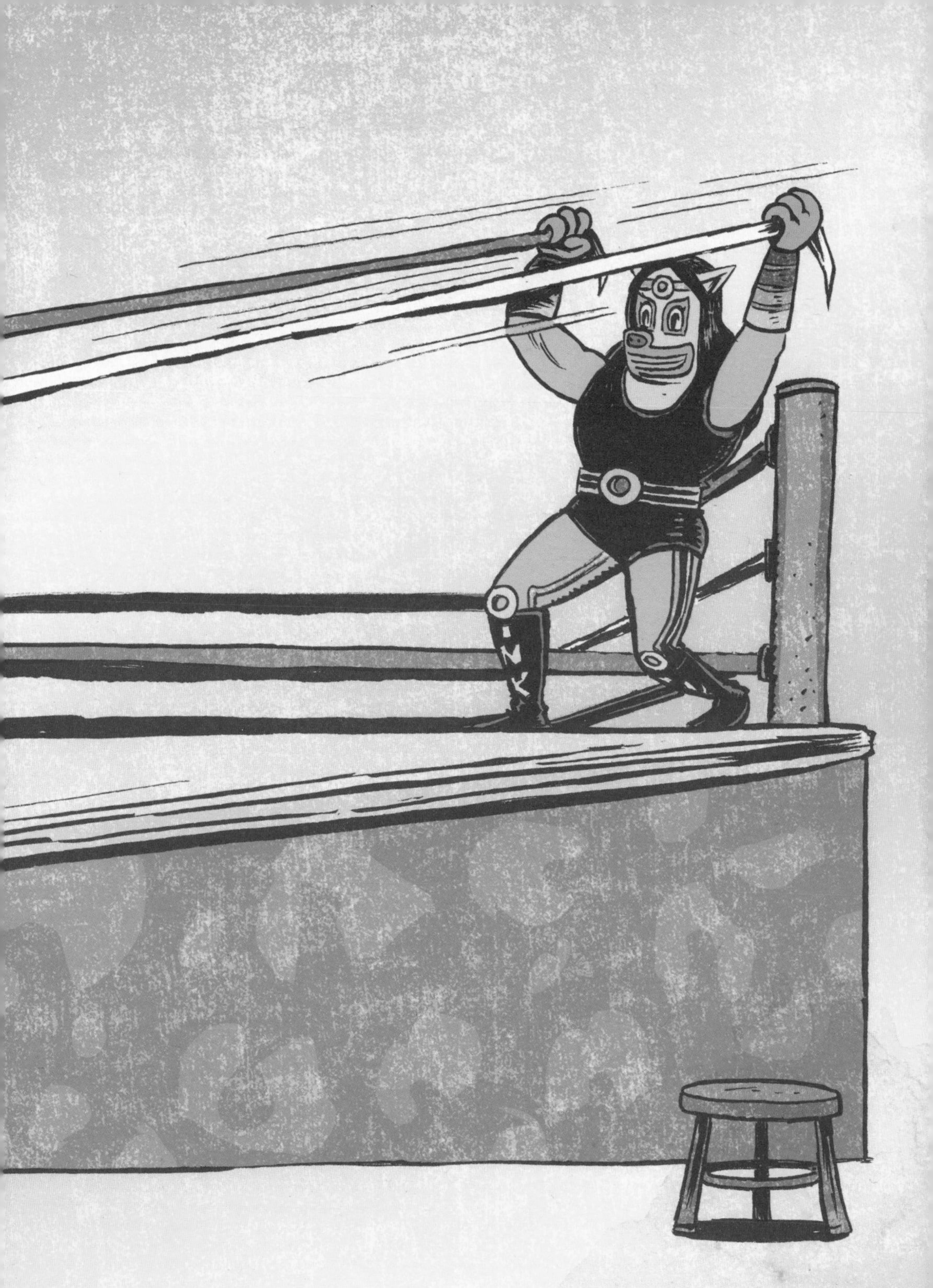
INK

El Toro washes the dishes.

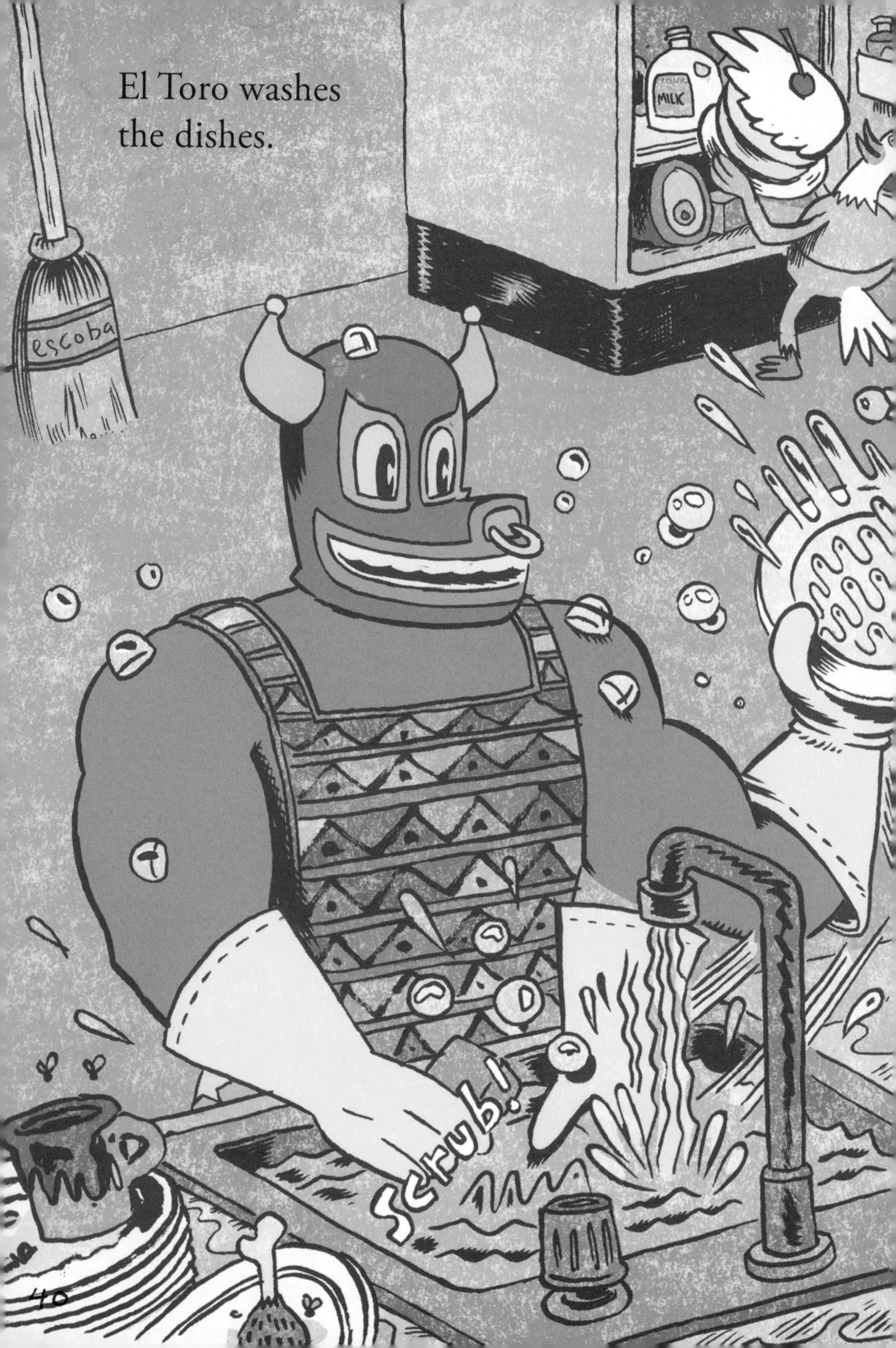
escoba
MILK
scrub!

La Oink Oink
blows them dry.

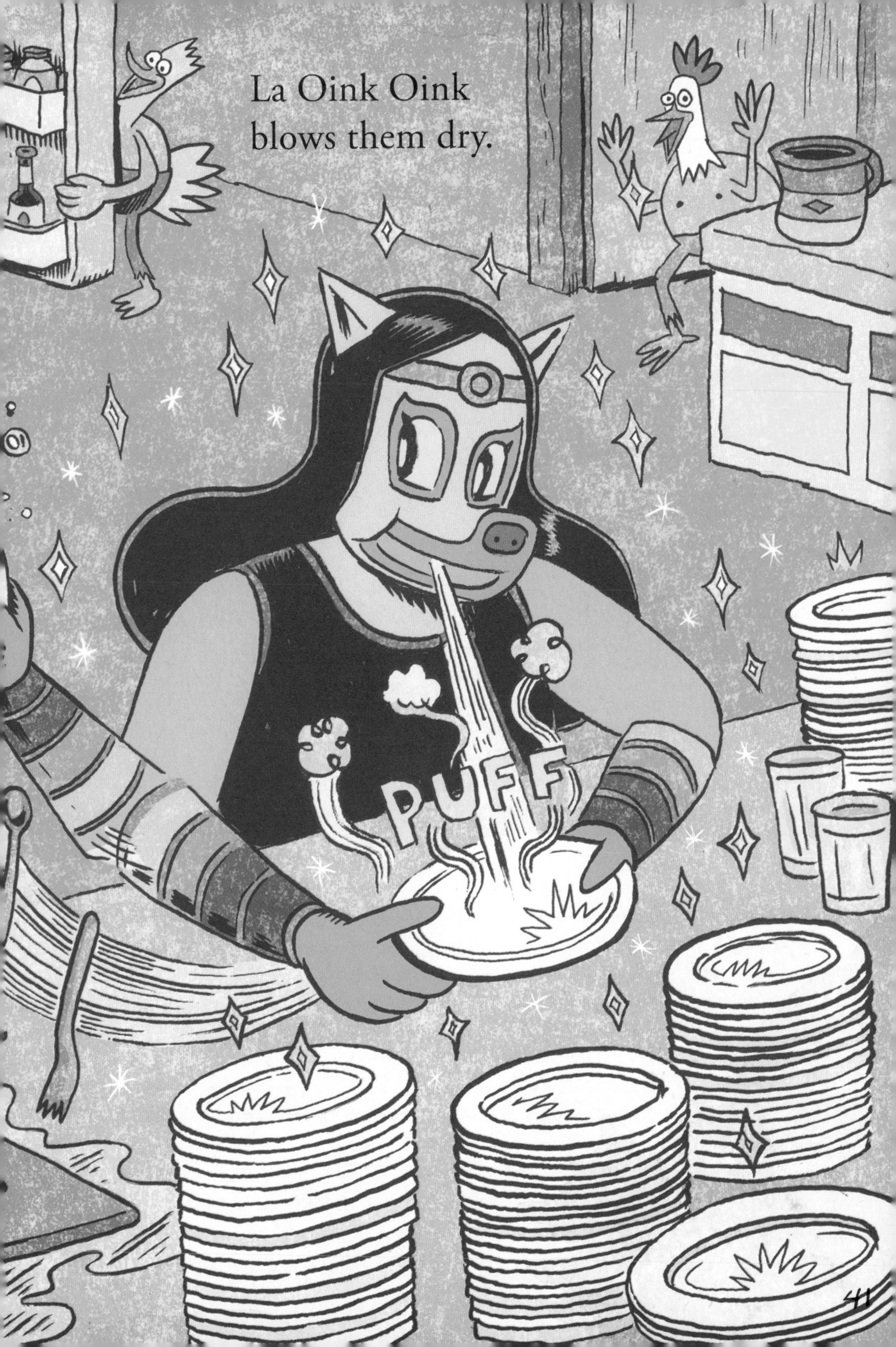
PUFF

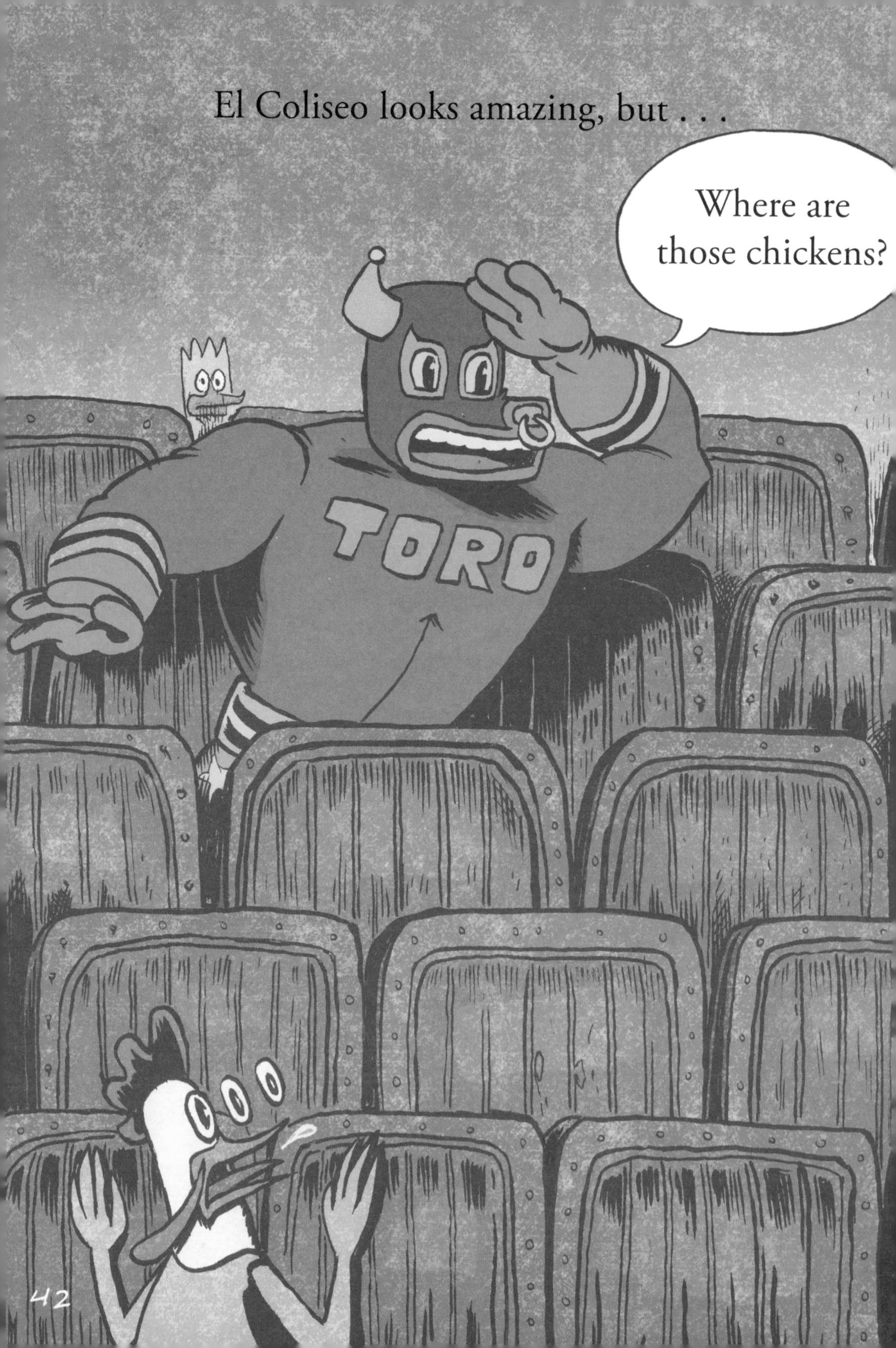
El Coliseo looks amazing, but . . .
Where are those chickens?
TORO

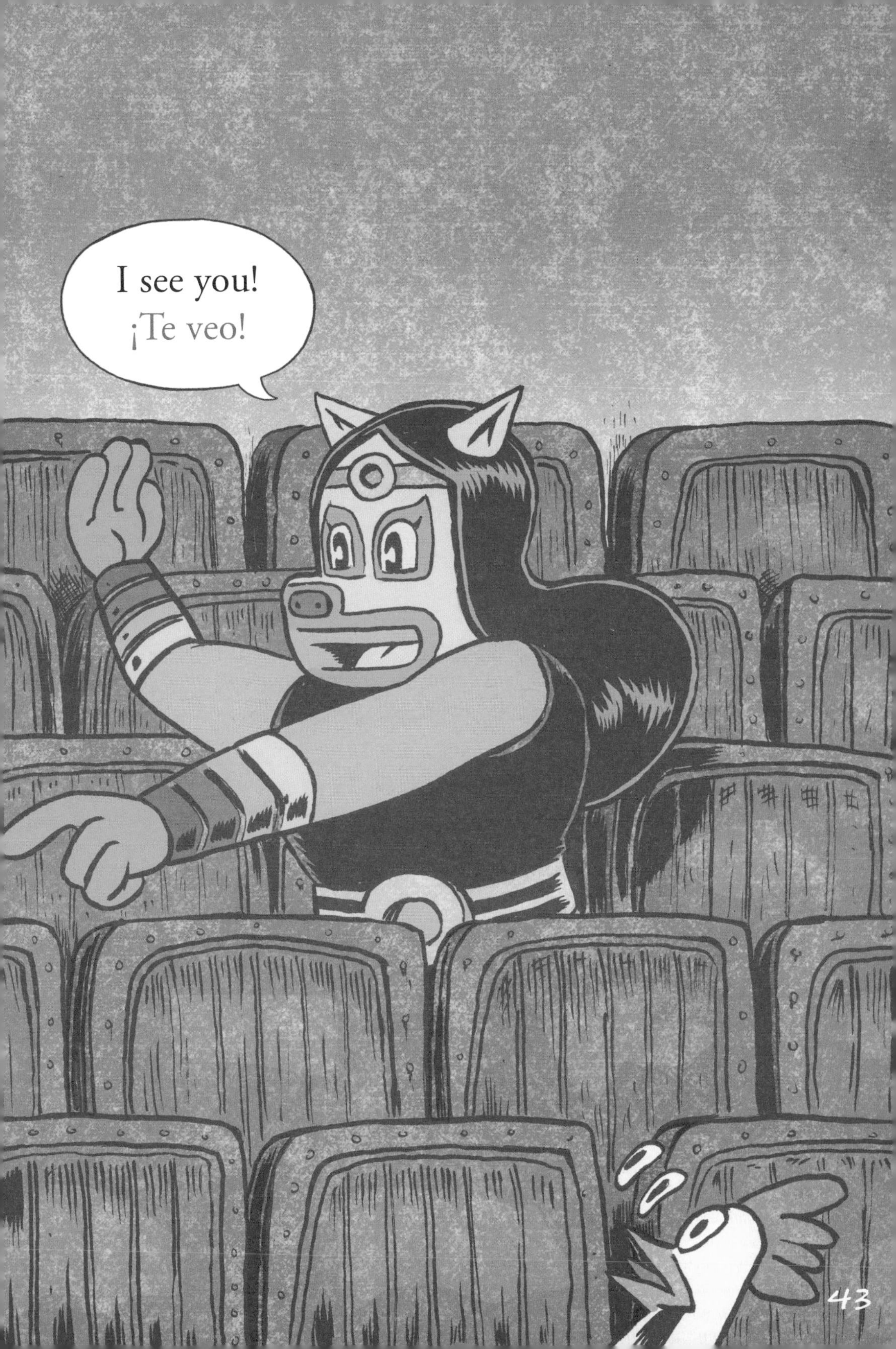
I see you!
¡Te veo!

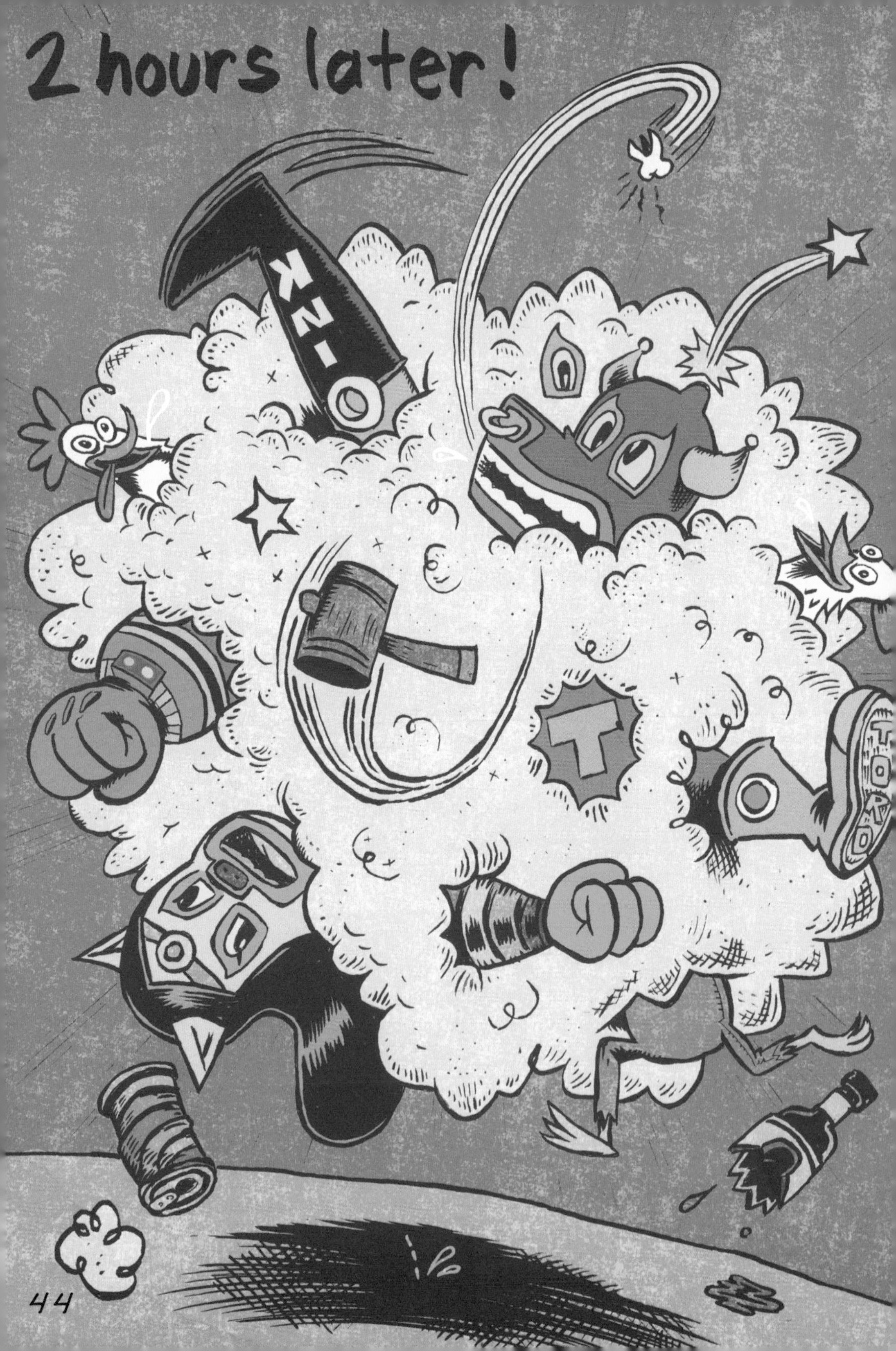
2 hours later!
INK
T
TORO

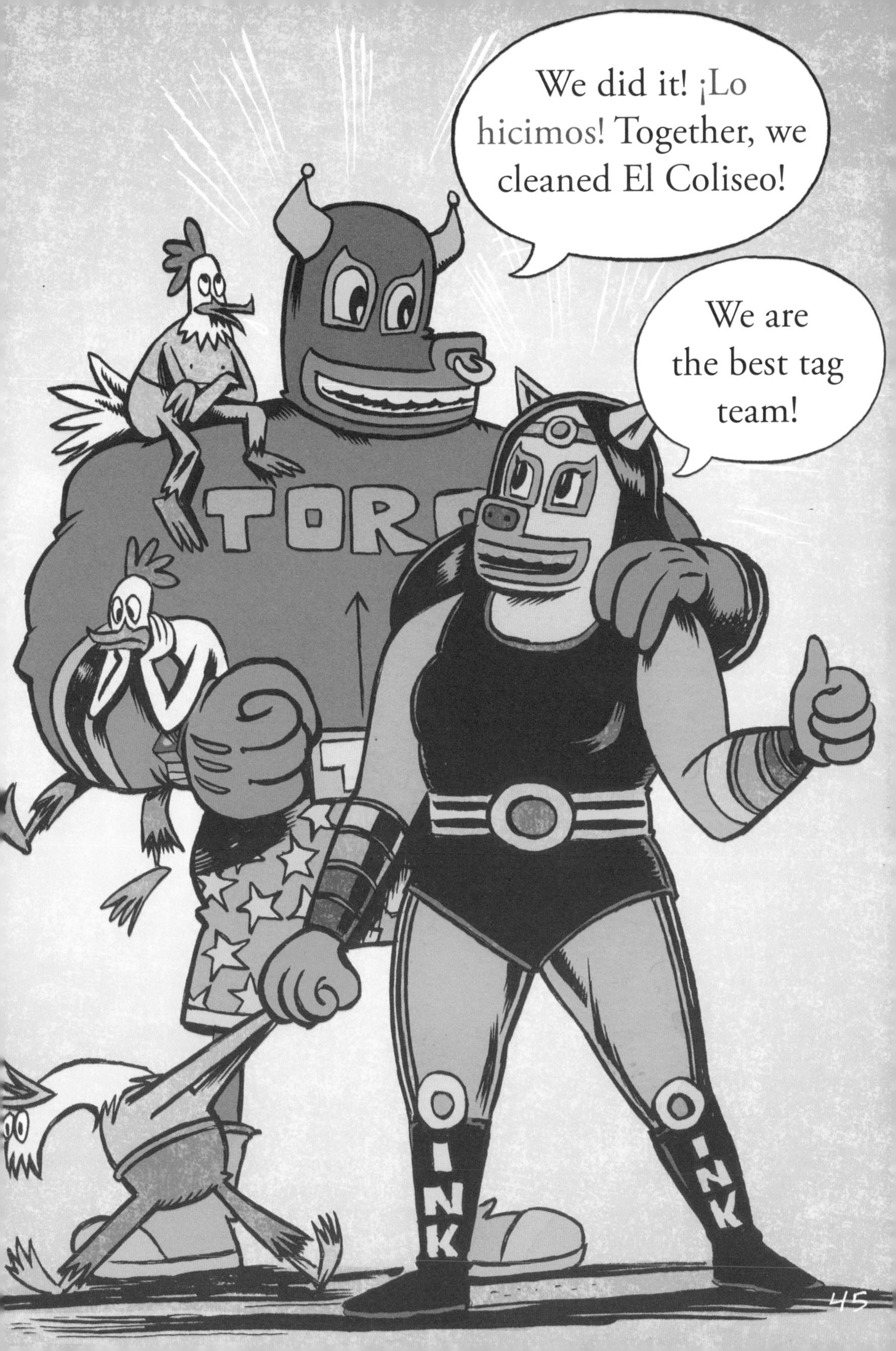
We did it! ¡Lo hicimos! Together, we cleaned El Coliseo!
We are the best tag team!
TORO
INK
INK

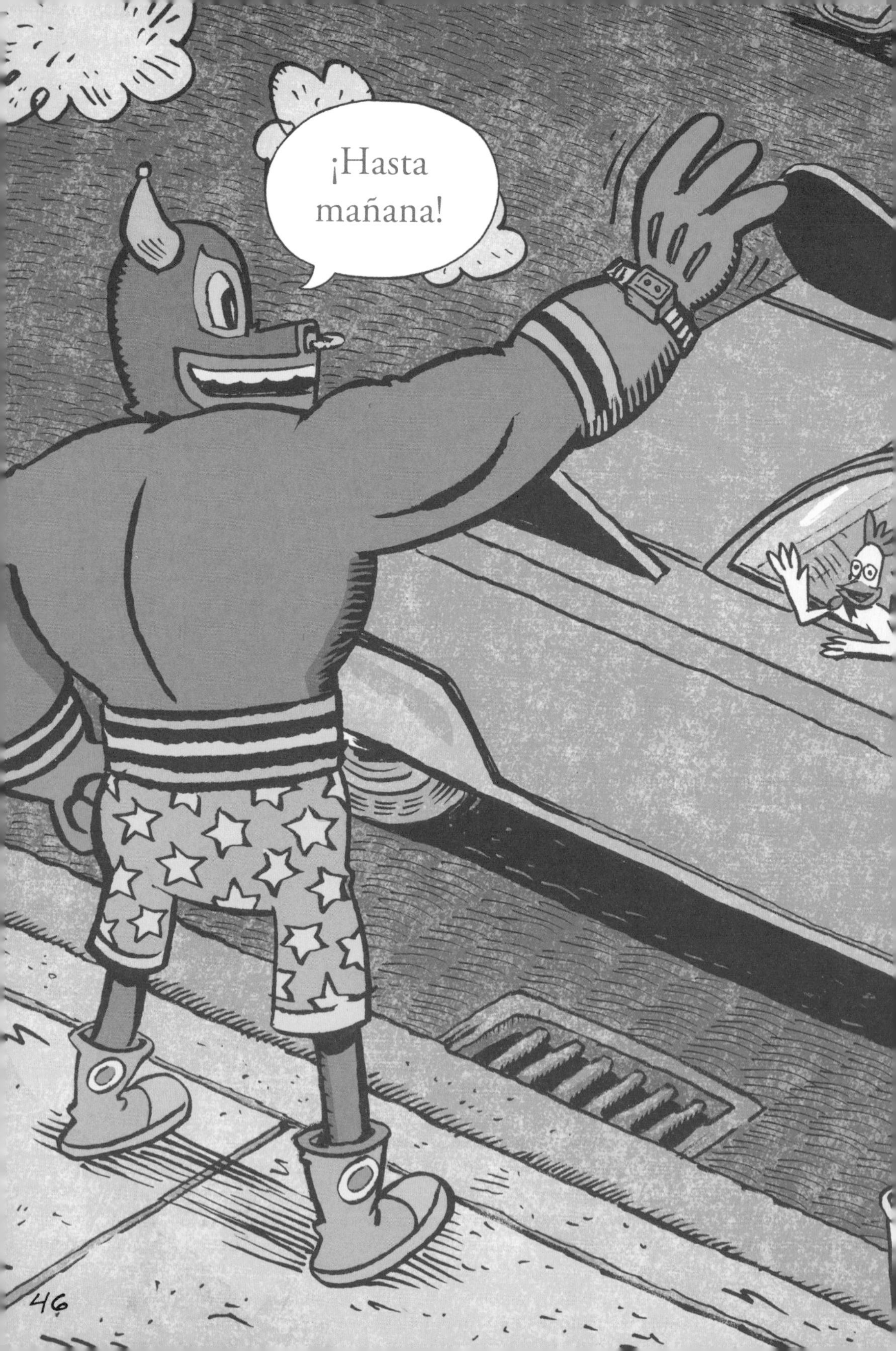
¡Hasta mañana!

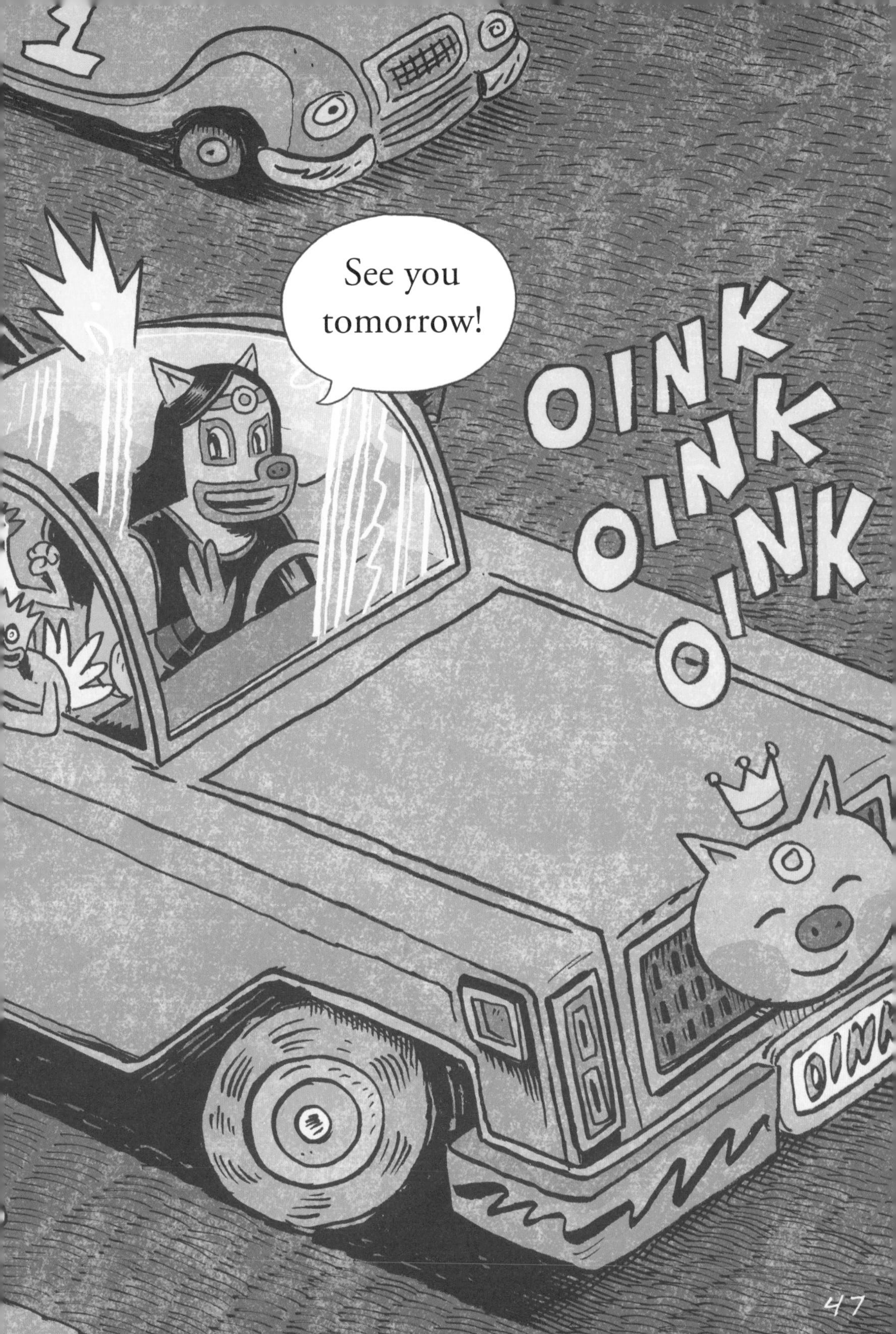
See you tomorrow!
OINK
OINK
OINK

To my spectacular tag team partner, Elaine.
You make my drawings look so good! —Raúl the Third

To my dedicated tag team partner, Raúl the Third.
I make your drawings look spectacular! —Elaine Bay

Versify® is an imprint of HarperCollins Publishers.
HarperAlley is an imprint of HarperCollins Publishers.

Tag Team
Copyright © 2021 by Raúl Gonzalez III
¡Vamos! is a registered trademark of Raúl Gonzalez.
All rights reserved. Manufactured in Malaysia. No part of this book may be
used or reproduced in any manner whatsoever without written permission
except in the case of brief quotations embodied in critical articles and
reviews. For information address HarperCollins Children's Books, a division
of HarperCollins Publishers, 195 Broadway, New York, NY 10007.
www.harperalley.com

Library of Congress Control Number: 2023943300
ISBN 978-0-06-335923-9

The artists used pen and ink on smooth plate Bristol board to create the
illustrations for this book. Colors were created with Adobe Photoshop.
Hand lettering by Raúl Gonzalez III
Design by Natalie Fondriest
24 25 26 27 28   COS   10 9 8 7 6 5 4 3 2 1

First paperback edition, 2024

Let's go back to El Coliseo and see if El Toro still needs our help.

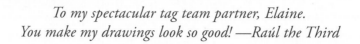